Relative Disenchantment

Patricia Shinn Wojtowicz

&

Christine Petersen Streed

Cover art by Christine Petersen Streed

ISBN: 1542640229
ISBN-13: 978-1542640220

Dedication

In loving memory of our grandmothers:

Anna, Eunice, Fanny, and Mary

Chapter 1

The dark November sky forecasted snow as Joanna slipped out of the Tech building, yet not even the dreary weather could deter her from her need to get away. In her rush to leave the lab, she had left everything behind, including her coat. Joanna shuddered.

As she neared Lake Michigan, the late afternoon light glistened on the icy shoreline. Ignoring the cold, Joanna climbed over the concrete slabs that separated the university from the lake. The gray sky blended with the steel-colored water, blurring the horizon. Gazing out over the enormous watery expanse, Joanna shivered partly from the cold, but mostly because she felt so hopeless. She crumpled down on a chunk of cement that jutted out over the water, hung her head and hugged her knees to her chest.

"I'm such a loser!" she wailed. Self-pity engulfed her as she cradled her head in her hands. *Some kind of doctor I'll be!*

Normally, neuro lab was the highlight of Joanna's week, but today she had witnessed something grim. Remembering how the TA had inserted the tiny patient's head into the guillotine, Joanna cringed. There were no ceremonious shouts of "Off with its head!" no final cigarette or meal, only the shiny blade swiftly dropping, instantly severing the subject's head from its body.

"This rat just lost its head to science," the TA had joked, prompting nervous laughter from Joanna's classmates.

Joanna shuddered again as she pictured the grisly scene.

And so now, here she sat at the edge of Lake Michigan. Overcome by frustration and self-doubt, a loud growl escaped from her throat. "Why can't I be a hard-ass like everybody else?" she yelled out. A tear rolled down one cheek. *I love neuroscience, but not if it means committing murder in order to learn.*

Craving a sense of calm, she rubbed her eyes and focused on the sound of the water lapping on the rocks beneath her feet.

Catching sight of a single leaf floundering in the waves, she watched as the leaf was pushed then pulled, closer to and then farther from the shore. She felt an affinity for the leaf's struggle. "Come on little guy, you can do it," she willed the leaf forward. But, its effort against the rough autumn waves was futile. She shook her fist as she called out to the leaf, "*Illegitimi non carborundum*!" remembering her Grandpa Jackman teaching her the Latin phrase for "Don't let the bastards grind you into the dirt."

Seemingly unchanged by the fervor of Joanna's plea, the leaf continued hopelessly. "Meh, What do I know? Do what you want." Looking for her phone to check the time, she sighed, "Oh crap!" Hauling herself up, she trudged back toward campus.

Chapter 2

Joanna shivered as she tugged at the door to the lab, relieved to find it still open. Snuggling into her coat, she felt for her phone. Momentarily elated that it was still in her coat pocket, she checked its screen only to see several missed calls from her newly-divorced mother. "Now what?" Feeling overwhelmed and hungry, Joanna stuffed her phone back into her pocket and headed off toward the cafeteria with the hope of securing a late dinner. A queasy feeling mingled with the gnawing in her stomach. The grisly scene in lab was partly to blame, but the uneasy feeling was a familiar one.

The news of her parents break-up had not surprised Joanna. They had been bickering for most of her life. As their only child, she did her best to be supportive, but as a stressed out pre-med student it was wearing on her. Every day she received a barrage of inane phone calls and texts from her father, Peter, and from her mother, Beverly, she got invitations, which Joanna knew were really commands in disguise. She loved her parents, but their unending neediness was getting to her. She sighed helplessly, *You guys really need to leave me alone.*

Reaching the cafeteria, Joanna noticed her roommate at a table near the entrance, sitting amid open books and a half-eaten dinner. Ear buds in, Deborah was bobbing her head, seemingly more interested in what was on her iPod than in her coursework.

Joanna grabbed an adjacent chair and smiled weakly at Deborah who returned her grin with a deep smile and a one-armed bear hug.

"Hey, JoJo Bean!" Deborah exclaimed, removing her earbuds. "Cute sweater! Is that new?"

"It is, thanks! I've been trying to find something in this color for a while."

"Nice! And it goes great with *my* boots." Deborah joked.

Joanna smiled. "Yeah, I get the hint. You can borrow it."

Even though she and Deborah appeared to have nothing in common, the girls had hit it off immediately after randomly being assigned as roommates in their freshman year.

"So, how was your day, Joanna?"

"Fine, I guess," Joanna responded. "How was yours?"

"Incredible!" Deborah beamed. "Aced my econ test, finished my essay for rhetoric, and did 50 laps in the pool. And, if that's not enough fabulousness for one day, I got an intriguing text from that cute guy I was telling you about in my anatomy lab."

"Sounds like a good..." Joanna started, but was interrupted by another phone call. "Sorry, Deb, I gotta take this. She's been calling me all day."

"Hi, Mom," Joanna answered flatly, and then was silent while she listened.

"You want what, Mom?" Joanna cringed, listening further.

"When?" Joanna's face wore a scowl as she tried to speak. "But..."

Unable to comment, Joanna's scowl became a frown as she shook her head. "But, Mom, tomorrow night isn't...."
More listening, then "Ok. Fine, Mom. See you then."

Joanna hung up. "How would you like a free gourmet meal tomorrow night, Deb?"

"Are you kidding me?" Deborah returned, poking at the congealed casserole on her plate. "Anything to get away from this dorm food!"

"Then, you are cordially invited to accompany me to Madame Beverly's fifty-third birthday party tomorrow night. Black tie optional."

The next evening as they rode the Metra to Wilmette, Deborah slumped over onto Joanna's shoulder and napped as Joanna sat rigidly in her seat, legs crossed with her right foot agitatedly tapping the air. She gnawed at her fingers and spat bits of detached nail and cuticle absent-mindedly across the train. There were only three stops between Evanston and Wilmette, but with each one, Joanna felt her campus life slipping a little further away -

along with her independence. As she neared her mother's home, Joanna could feel herself shrinking under the certain maternal scrutiny to come.

So absorbed was she in her own thoughts, Joanna nearly missed the Wilmette stop, managing at the last possible minute to rouse Deborah and dash toward the exit.

Deborah yawned and rubbed her eyes. "I can't believe I fell asleep," she said more to herself than to Joanna. "But man, do I have to pee!" She yawned again and stretched, then scurried after Joanna who was already exiting the platform.

In silence, the two friends walked the three blocks to Joanna's childhood home. Although Joanna was not in any mood to celebrate with her mother, she smiled at Deborah whose excitement was evident by the way her mouth gaped open as they passed the elegant homes on the tree-lined streets of Wilmette.

Turning a corner, Joanna said. "That's it over there," as she pointed toward the massive red brick Georgian home at the end of the street. Even in November, the perfectly manicured lawn was apparent. The front walkway leading up to the palatial facade was flanked on each side with a tight, low, immaculately trimmed hedge. The ivy climbing the brick exterior seemed as though it had been trained to arch and bend in just the right places.

Deborah stopped dead in her tracks, giggled and then yelled, "Wow!"

Ascending the stairs to the front porch, Joanna reached for the doorknob and flinched. Beverly's extravaganza was about to begin. *Mom always loves a good show.* A deep sense of dread pervaded her whole body, threatening to ruin the entire evening.

In contrast, Deborah stood gaping at the massive front door with its beveled sidelights. "This is the kind of house you see in the movies, but you don't believe that real people actually live in them."

Sighing, Joanna held the front door open for Deborah, and then forced herself to enter the house. "Mom, we're here," she announced, trying to sound enthusiastic, while feeling anything but.

"Wow! This is where you grew up, Jo?!" Deborah exclaimed, prancing around in the foyer as she took in the grandeur of the house. "I think I'm going to wet my pants!"

"Yep, this is where I grew up. Cold-sterile-don't-get-anything-dirty Wilmette."

"No, I mean I really gotta pee," Deborah interjected.

Joanna directed her friend to the large powder room off of the foyer. Hearing a bleep from her coat, she checked her phone. It was another call from her dad - making a total of three for the day. *Geez, Dad. I know you're lonely now that you're on your own, but I'm not a counselor.* She hit ignore, her usual response to her father's calls lately. Stepping back out onto the front porch, she dialed her voicemail.

"You have one new voice message."

Then, "Hi, Pumpkin. It's Dad. Just wanted to let you know that Chase Elliott came in second last night. Chase shoulda' won, but Carl Edwards beat him out at the last minute. But, at least I got to see Carl do his signature backflip after his win. Wish you could've seen it with me. Guess that's all. Miss you and love you. Give me a call sometime."

"Good to know, Dad," she said dryly as she deleted the message.

Joanna could not remember a time when her dad, a freelance sports writer who worked from home, had not been fascinated with motor sports. However, since her parents' divorce, his interest had become an obsession. For her father's sake, Joanna had feigned an interest in what her mother liked to call "redneck recklessness." But, as her father floundered in his new status as a single, white male, his inane calls to Joanna about racing had gotten out of hand, so much so that Joanna had finally given up answering or even returning her dad's calls. And sadly, Joanna had noticed that while his knowledge of racing increased, his writing productivity suffered. On the other hand, Joanna's mother, always the workaholic, had thrown herself even more so into her high-profile real estate business.

Thoughts of her mother brought her back. Grabbing the doorknob to the front door, Joanna took a deep breath and willed herself to feel excited about her mother's party. As she re-entered the house, she noticed the powder room door was ajar. "Deb?" There was no answer, which prompted Joanna to scan the rooms she could see from the foyer. No sign of Deborah. In the sprawling Jackman house, it was easy to lose track of people.

Suddenly, distracted by voices coming from the back of the house, Joanna temporarily gave up her search for Deborah and stepped into the large living room in an effort to monitor the conversation drifting toward her. She recognized the voices as those belonging to her mother and some of her mother's closest friends, but could not make out the details of the discussion.

Still not ready to be a part of the evening's festivities, Joanna stood awkwardly in the living room, eavesdropping while trying not to melt into the perfection that was her mother's home. The showroom quality of each piece of furniture seemed to emphasize her rough edges all the more. Joanna pulled at the strings of her oversized hoodie, feeling self-conscious about her choice of attire. Normally, she would have worn a dress and heels for this type of occasion. However, she had specifically chosen to wear the hoodie, skinny jeans, and clunky boots with the hope of irritating her mother.

She knew her ensemble emphasized her muscular build, which was still present from her years on the high school swim team. Her long brown hair hung across her face, hiding a brow that sported a concerning number of lines considering her mere 20 years of life—a feature she had acquired from environment more than genetics.

With the heavily bitten fingernails of one hand, she picked at a hangnail on the other hand as she slunk across the living room and peeked into the family room. Hovering at a distance, she took in the scene, noticing her mother dressed in a crisp, white suit with her smooth hair highlighted bronze.

Something bothering you, Mom? Joanna wondered as she watched her mother's mouth set itself into what Joanna perceived as a firm line of judgment. Realizing that Beverly's eyes had come to rest on her, Joanna felt her mother scanning her from head to toe. Joanna grimaced. *I know Mom. My hair hangs in my face and you can see my knees right through my jeans. Hope North Shore Magazine's not here for another photo shoot.* Joanna thought sarcastically.

Only Joanna sensed her mother's suppressed sigh, before she heard, "Oh, here's Joanna." Joanna forced a smile as her mother drew her into the room.

Her entry prompted Millie, her mother's best friend, to walk over, lips pursed, ready to plant air kisses on Joanna. *Ugh! I hate fake kisses.* Unfazed by Joanna's aversion, Millie grazed Joanna's cheek with her own and abruptly turned away. "Oh, Beverly, did you hear? Steven just pledged Jonathon's fraternity," she bragged breathily.

Her mother shot back a jealousy-tinged rebuttal, "Well, Joanna doesn't have time for the sorority scene…"

Joanna scoffed softly to herself. *Yeah, right. How about— Joanna wasn't part of the sorority scene because she wouldn't be caught dead in a sorority house.*

Beverly continued. "...because she's doing so well in her pre-med studies."

Joanna shuddered at the continued bragging of the two mothers, which was quickly becoming just an annoying rivalry. *Oh, just shoot me now!*

Then from across the family room, a peal of laughter sounded causing Joanna to turn and see Deborah leaning in closer to Steven. He whispered something in her friend's ear. *Is she blushing?*

"Joanna! I'm talking to you," said Beverly. "Tell Millie about your medical experience at the nursing home during the summer."

She bit on a loose flap of cuticle and tore the skin away with her teeth, leaving an open, raw spot. "Oh, you mean calling Bingo?" Joanna answered sarcastically.

Beverly glared at Joanna, but before she could say anything Millie changed the subject back to Steven.

This scene seemed to Joanna to be straight out of a nightmare. *Can this get any worse?* She glanced down to see if she was naked.

Suddenly, a hand grabbed hers, pulling it away from her mouth. "Don't chew your fingers," said Deborah.

"That's what you say to me after I brought you to my home for dinner?" Joanna glared at her. "You sound just like my mother." She guided Deborah toward one corner of the room with her hands on her friend's arm.

Deborah looked at Joanna with a puzzled frown. "Sorry, but I hate to see you so undone by a family event."

Joanna whispered, "So what was going on between you and Steven over there?"

"Boy, he's a phony, isn't he?"

Joanna smirked. "Oh, yeah. *He's* the phony."

"Hey! Unfair! I was just talking to him." She gently removed Joanna's hands from her arm.

Another snippet of conversation was tossed their way, "Has Joanna decided to which medical schools she'll be applying?" causing Joanna to pull Deborah by the sleeve, leading her toward the dining room before the gut-wrenching details of her life were exposed.

The scents of roast beef and freshly baked bread hung in the house, intensifying as the two friends moved into the dining room. Lavish place settings gleamed on the dining room table.

"What's wrong?" Deborah asked.

"I feel like the *real* phony." Joanna sighed. "There's irony for you."

Deborah patted Joanna's arm. "Come on, it's a party. Forget about school for today. I'm ready for some good food!"

Chapter 3

Joanna chose seats at the far end of the table knowing that Beverly would take the seat at the head of the table. *Dad's seat,* thought Joanna as she sat, pulling her napkin from its ring and placing it in her lap. Millie and Jonathon, the friends Beverly had won in the divorce, sat to each side of Beverly, while Joanna sat, flanked by Deborah and Steven. Taking a gulp of water from the goblet in front of her, Joanna steeled herself for the *grand event.*

A waiter arrived from the kitchen with a tray, placing several bowls on the table in front of Beverly. "Shall we begin?" she announced.

"First, a toast," said Jonathon. He raised his wine glass to Beverly. Everyone at the table lifted a glass. "Many happy returns. May you stay this gorgeous for many more birthdays."

Joanna resisted the urge to smirk as Beverly smiled and sipped her wine. "Thank you, Jonathon. Let's dine while it's still hot, shall we?" she said, passing a bowl of green beans almondine to her right.

The clinking of dishes prevailed during the passing of bowls and the filling of plates.

"This all looks delicious," said Jonathon, picking up his fork.

As Millie tucked into her meal, she asked, "Beverly, how is your mother?"

Even with the distance between them, Joanna could hear the sigh escape her mother's lips before she said, "She's doing as well as can be expected. She's just getting forgetful and…more unpredictable." Beverly sliced the juicy roast beef on her plate.

"What do you mean?" asked Millie, leaning forward in her chair with anticipation.

Another sigh. "She got a dog."

"What's so bad about that?"

"The dog is large, the house is small, and the first week he was there, she tripped over him and fell." Gripping her wine glass, Beverly shook her head. "It was just some bruises, but the next time could be worse."

Millie patted her hand. "Don't worry, Teddy will take care of her."

"Oh, yeah, right," Beverly scoffed. "You know how irresponsible Teddy is. He can barely take care of himself." She sipped from her glass. "All I can say is he'd better get that dog out of the house if he knows what's good for him."

"Teddy is an odd one. I'll give you that. But, surely he wants what's best for your mother." Millie countered.

"Good point, Millie. But, Teddy's weird sense of the world doesn't always translate to safety."

Rapidly losing her appetite as she listened to the verbal exchange at the other end of the table, Joanna poked at her mashed potatoes. She found it nearly impossible to block out her mother's voice even with the conversation between Deborah and Steven buzzing away right next to her.

Deborah nudged her. "Hey, this is the best roast beef I've ever had."

"Well, of course it is. Mom slaved over it for days. She had to call three caterers to make this dinner happen."

Deborah laughed. "Believe me. This is not my first catered dinner. At my house, The Coronel cooks for us all the time."

"Well, I'm glad this meal makes you feel at home."

Suddenly Joanna sensed that she had become the topic of conversation yet again at the other end of the table. "Joanna just needs to try new things," Millie paused to finish the wine in her glass. "She should make social events more of a priority."

Joanna ceremoniously pushed back her chair, stood, and announced, "My tolerance for opinions has been fully satisfied." Removing her plate from the table, she slipped into the kitchen where she plopped the plate into the half-filled sink, turned on the hot water, and squirted a generous supply of Ivory soap into the greasy mess. She watched the expanding mound of bubbles in the sink as it filled.

"Miss, I'll take care of that," said the waiter.

"No, it's okay. I'd like to wash a few dishes. Thanks."

He shrugged and moved off to prepare for dessert.

Joanna felt something brush her arm. "Can I help?" asked Deborah, standing at her side.

"If you want to." Joanna leaned against the sink lost for a moment in her own thoughts. "This is my favorite part of a dinner party."

"What? Working off all the excessive calorie intake?"

"No. Well, maybe that. But I always like getting away from the crowd." She scrubbed at the pot that contained the mashed potatoes. "When I was a kid, we used to go to New Jersey to visit Grandma. After dinner, she and I would go into the kitchen and do the dishes while everyone else slouched on the couch, napping, digesting, and watching football. I always had the best talks with my grandma while she rinsed the dishes and I dried them."

Suddenly, Deborah turned to Joanna and excitedly suggested, "Hey, you should call her."

"That's a great idea!" Joanna dried her hands. "And, I can do even better than that. I'll be right back."

She returned with a laptop and placed it on the counter. "I wonder if my Nutty Uncle Teddy will be on-line. Who am I kidding…He's always on-line!"

"Hey, everyone," Joanna announced as she positioned the laptop on the dining table in the place her plate had occupied during the meal. "Grandma is here for the party!" She angled the computer screen to face the center of the table, and then sat down with the crowd to converse with her grandmother.

There sat Ruth in her housedress, crookedly buttoned, revealing more cleavage than she had most likely intended. Her white hair was smashed flat on one side. "Hello, Grandma," Joanna said at the computer screen. "Can you see us?"

"Well, hello dear," Ruth replied looking around as if confused by where Joanna's voice was coming from.

"Look right here," came a deep and somewhat wheezy male voice from off screen. "I'll make the picture full-screen."

"Oh Teddy, well isn't that just amazing," said Ruth, leaning forward, talking at the computer's camera as if it were a microphone, giving those seated at Beverly's table an intimate view up the inside of her right nostril.

"No, you don't talk there. That's the camera. Look at this picture here and you can see them," came Teddy's somewhat irritated voice.

"Oh, okay," Ruth replied uncertainly while she acknowledged the advice and backed away from the web-cam. "Oh, there you all are." Her face lit up. "Hello, everyone," she said cheerily, looking intently at the picture on her screen. "Happy birthday Beverly, dear. Wish I could be there with all of you." Ruth waved at the image of her family on her computer, revealing more of an unintentional peek at her cleavage.

Beverly sat at the head of the table, stiffly. "Hello Mother," she replied with a hint of ice in her voice. "You might want to button up your robe."

"I got it," came Teddy's voice. And suddenly, two hairy arms appeared from the right side of the screen.

"What are you eating today, Grandma?" asked Joanna.

"Oh my, what a feast. We ran over to the Wegman's last night and picked us up two Swanson Fried Chicken Dinners and a Sara Lee pumpkin pie."

"Sounds yummy, Grandma. We had our dinner catered – right down to the cloth napkins and horse de vors." Joanna purposely mispronounced 'hors d'oeuvres' as she shot a spiteful glance at her mother.

"Well, now that sounds downright fancy, dear."

Joanna sat back and watched the various interactions between her grandmother and the others seated at the table. She detected a bit of deflation on her mother's face and almost felt sorry for her, but as Joanna watched, Beverly's face suddenly hardened, her mouth set in a firm line. Joanna scanned back to the laptop screen to see what her mother was seeing.

Ruth was no longer visible. Something black and blurry had obscured the view. Just as Joanna was about to ask Nutty Uncle Teddy what was going on, Beverly left the table, cell phone in hand. Then, Joanna detected the tune "Wasting Away Again in Margaritaville" intermixed with the conversation coming from her laptop. The fuzzy, black interference moved, allowing Joanna to discern its nature.

Deborah gasped. "Oh, he's sooo cute! What's his name?" A large black Labrador Retriever bobbed up and down at the bottom of the screen, trying to get attention from Ruth.

From the kitchen, Beverly whispered loudly, "Teddy, what the hell is that dog still doing there?"

Then, from the background of Ruth's kitchen, and picked up by the laptop speaker: "Hey! Why are you calling my cell phone? You know you can just talk to me by Skype."

A rush of anxiety hit Joanna. Teddy had always been weird, and his behavior seemed to irritate Beverly so much that she was rarely in a good mood when she spoke to him. *I hope Grandma doesn't figure out what is going on and get caught in the crossfire,* thought Joanna, gnawing on her fingernail.

Ruth stroked the large puppy's head despite the dog's incessant bouncing. "This is Peanut. Say hello Peanut."

From the kitchen Joanna heard Beverly say through clenched teeth, "Yes, I know that. I'd rather not upset our happy occasion by ripping into you in front of Mom. Why is that damn dog still there?"

While Deborah baby-talked to Peanut, Joanna strained to hear Teddy's response through the laptop.

"Wow! That's some mouth you got on you." And then apparently oblivious to Beverly's furious demeanor, Teddy added,

"Hey Bevie, what's another name for a beaver?" Without leaving any time for Beverly to respond, Teddy whispered, "Pause for comic effect." Then instantly answered his own question "A dam dog. Get it? A dam dog… you know without the 'n'."

"Teddy, stop with your stupid jokes for once! This is serious!" said Beverly.

Joanna scanned the faces of those still seated around the table in an attempt to determine if anyone else was hearing the background conversation. If they did, they didn't show any sign of it. The dog seemed to have captivated everyone's attention for the moment, so Joanna decided to use the distraction. "Aww, Grandma, you got a dog! How did you come up with the name Peanut?"

Upon hearing his name, the excited puppy woofed directly into the laptop microphone, causing everyone to cringe at the volume.

Ruth seemed unperturbed by the noise. "Well, reminds me of your dog, dear, only smaller. How is Duke?"

"Um. Gram, Duke's been gone now for over a year."

"Oh, too bad. You will all just have to come out for a visit and meet Peanut." Peanut placed his paws on Ruth's shoulder and licked the side of her face, knocking off her glasses. "That's my little Pea-pea!" she clucked in response.

But despite everyone's fascination with Peanut, Joanna was still well aware of the phone conversation transpiring between her mother and uncle

"Teddy, don't lose my point. Get rid of that dog," hissed Beverly.

"Okay. Okay. It's not as easy as it sounds."

"Well, as far as I can recall, you don't have a job, so it seems to me like you should have plenty of time to take care of it. I'm going to call in a week. If that thing isn't gone…" Beverly's voice trailed off.

"But, Mom really likes him."

"Mom also likes being able to walk. If she trips over that dog and breaks something, that burden will be on you."

"You worry too much. I won't let that happen."

"Well, you don't worry enough. Now act like an adult and take on some responsibility for once. I've said what I have to say."

Ending the call, Beverly reappeared in the dining room, announcing that it was time for dessert. "I'm sorry, but we have to hang up, Mother." Beverly stalked back into the kitchen.

Joanna could tell that Beverly wasn't sorry at all, and the disappointment was obvious in Ruth's voice as she said, "Okay, if you say so, dear."

"Bye, Grandma. It was great talking to you, but I wish we could all be together for the holidays," Joanna said trying to cheer her up.

Beverly returned with dessert plates and forks, forcefully depositing the dishes on the table, sending the forks a-clutter on top of the plates.

Ruth perked up. "Yes, that would be nice. Maybe you can come to New Jersey for Christmas. It would be just like old times."

"Hey, Mom, what do you think?" Joanna shot a knowing glance at her mother.

Beverly scowled, reaching toward the computer.

As Joanna realized her mother's intent to end the call, she blurted out, "It was great seeing you, Grandma. We'll talk again soon. Bye now."

"Bye, now," came Ruth's farewell, followed by Teddy's, "So long. Happy Birth—

Beverly slammed the laptop shut.

Chapter 4

Back in her dorm, Joanna struggled to keep her eyelids from drooping. Exhausted by her family interactions, she fought the urge to sleep. The clock on her computer screen read 11:30, and she still had to write a lab report for neuroscience. Desperately, Joanna tried to focus on her work, then threw her hands in the air and muttered, "I can't think right now." A few minutes with her head down on the desk sounded enticing, so she set her phone to ring at midnight and pushed aside the clutter of papers. Using her neuroscience textbook as a pillow, she fell into a deep sleep.

Groggy after her short nap, Joanna yawned. Head still resting on the desk, she opened her eyes to see her completed lab report lying next to her. "Aw, cool! My paper is done!" Pushing the hair out of her eyes, she smirked in satisfaction at the callous title, "Neuroscience Lab 6: The Rat's Death Sentence."

Suddenly, she cringed as a sharp sensation on the back of her neck distracted her. Having perfected the desktop nap in her short college career, this crick in her neck surprised Joanna. But even more startling was the perception of cold metal trapping her against the desk. She massaged her neck, but any movement worsened the pain. Blindly groping the back of her head, she tried to make some sense of the situation. Running her hand up the metal, she found what seemed to be a blade suspended over her by a rope. An image formed in her mind: the hanging blade of a guillotine. She drew her hand back suddenly to avoid disturbing the blade. But then…Th-wack!

Joanna jerked her head up. Heart racing, eyes blinking, she puzzled at her roommate and the book that lay on the floor between their beds.

"Oh, sorry!" said Deborah. "Did I wake you?" But, the sly grin on her face told Joanna that she wasn't really sorry. "Don't you have a report due in the morning, sleepyhead?"

"Yup. It's right here…" Joanna boasted as she reached over to where she had seen it. But, it wasn't there. Shuffling through the papers, Joanna searched the desk for the report she believed she had written. Then the realization hit her: she had only dreamed it, and now it was nearly midnight and she was no closer to finishing her assignment than before her nap.

Feeling defeated, Joanna sank down in her chair. "Um. Just putting the finishing touches on it."

"Okay, well, I'm done for today. Don't stay up too late."

Deborah clicked off the overhead light, leaving the tiny dorm room illuminated only by the glow of Joanna's computer screen. Yawning, Joanna circled her shoulders, attempting to get serious about the work in front of her. But, she couldn't get her mind off the grisly details of the death she had witnessed in her neuroscience lab, thus the guilt-ridden dream put out by her subconscious.

Fingertips poised over her keyboard, Joanna waited for ideas to flow from her cortex to her computer, but she remained unfocused and thus unproductive. She stared at the blank screen again, then heaved a sigh and massaged her temples. A voice from deep in her right brain began to speak to her.

I'm that paper you were supposed to write yesterday. I've been rolling around in the back of your head, trying to spill out through your fingers onto the keyboard, but you've been stopping me. What's more important than me? So you're a little distracted. If you get me out of your head, there will be room for other things. C'mon! Just start typing.

"I know! I know!" Joanna said out loud.

BZZZ…BZZZ…Her cell phone sounded. Glancing at the screen, she was not surprised to see her father's smiling face beaming up at her. Worried about her dad's state of mind, Joanna reached over to answer her phone. But, then, thinking better of it, she hit "ignore." Although she felt guilty at disregarding her dad, she had work of her own to complete and did not have time to play counselor at this late hour of the night.

So, now, here she was, paper due, no inspiration, blank screen, clock ticking. *What do you mean no inspiration?* said her right brain. *I'm in here—just let me out!*

Feeling lost, incapable, and a little crazy, she thought, *I've written an A paper before. I can do it again.* She rubbed her eyes. *But not tonight. I'll wake up early.* She closed the lid of her laptop and muttered, "Screw it," as she climbed into bed.

The next morning after a rough night of tossing and turning, she hit the snooze button more than once. Finally by 7:30 Joanna was awake, although not quite cognizant. She had just enough time to shower, eat something, and make it to her first class—the class in which her non-existent paper was due. Fear of consequences combined with hunger pangs gripped her stomach. She reached for a chocolate Pop-Tart as she opened her computer and signed on, wishing she had not gone to sleep without finishing her assignment—knowing that she had. She typed out a cursory lab report, and then giving her armpits a quick sniff, she dressed and rushed out the door.

Chapter 5

With another rough day of classes behind her, Joanna slouched at the desk in her dorm room. Rubbing her forehead, she reprimanded herself for her procrastination. The lab report, written in haste that morning, had her worrying about her neurology grade. Annoyed with herself, and school, and life, she groaned, "Mom's gonna kill me."

"What'd you say?" Deborah asked, pulling her nose out of a book.

"My mom is going to kill me!"

"Yeah, I've met your mom. You're probably right," Deborah joked. "I've seen how your sweet grandma, your goofy uncle, and even a cute puppy can push her right over the edge."

"Ha, ha," Joanna replied sarcastically.

"Sorry, I couldn't help it." Deborah apologized. "Why specifically do you think she is going to kill you?"

"Oh, I don't know. My grades suck. My life sucks. I'll be lucky if I don't flunk out. She might as well kill me and put me out of my misery."

"Oh, don't worry. Your mom won't kill you. She hasn't gotten the full worth of her investment out of you yet." Deborah peered at Joanna over the top of her Econ textbook.

"Maybe I'll just have to put myself out of my misery," Joanna shot back.

"Oh, that would really show her," Deborah returned with a smirk.

"You're always so sarcastic! I can't talk to you about this now." Joanna pushed her chair away from the desk and stormed out of the small dorm room.

"Hey, come on! I was just joking!" Deborah called out following Joanna down the stairs. As Joanna was crossing through the foyer, Deborah caught up to her. "They're only grades, Joanna. It's been a tough quarter."

Joanna let out a huff of air as she jerked open the heavy front door. "Only grades! Those grades determine my future, Deborah, and I don't know what I'm going to do now." She ran down the front stairs, pushing past a group of chatting students and stormed off down the sidewalk.

"Where are you going?" Deborah hollered. "It's freezing out here, and you don't have your coat!"

"I don't know," Joanna spat back. "I need some time to think." Leaving Deborah behind, Joanna barely escaped being flattened by an oncoming car as she crossed the street. She started to run, but hours of studying over the past quarter had left her flabby and short-winded. Panting and out of breath, her pace slowed, but she continued to walk, making her way across Sheridan Road and finally stopping when she reached Lake Michigan.

Inundated by thoughts of failure, Joanna sat down on a sloping slab of concrete. As she considered her pathetic existence, she noticed another tiny leaf being pushed about by the strong lake current. Mesmerized by the leaf's futile attempts to reach shore, she wondered if it was the same leaf she had seen just days before.

Wiggling her frigid toes, she knew it was time to get up and moving, but she just couldn't ignore the little leaf bobbing helplessly in the current. As she watched the leaf's never-ending struggle against the forces of nature, Joanna lunged for the leaf and said, "I'll save you!"

Suddenly, out of balance, she teetered forward, sliding then plunging headfirst into the dark water. A sharp pain exploded in her head as she grazed a rocky surface hidden below the water. She found herself face up, floating in the bone-chilling waves.

Gasping at the cold, she tried to drag herself up, but her sweater, heavy with the frigid water, dragged her down. She kicked her feet and found they were so cold she could no longer feel them. A scream escaped and sputtered from her lips, then was silenced by a wave of water that slapped her in the face. Desperately, she grabbed for something to hold onto. Flailing against the water, she grasped at the rocky edge of the shore and pulled with all her strength. Her arms ached, her lungs burned, but she grabbed again and kicked with her numb feet until she finally got a strong enough hold on the rocks to inch herself up out of the water. With no strength left, she collapsed on the cold, hard shoreline.

Shivering uncontrollably, Joanna sensed the security of sheets and blankets around her. Then, there was Deborah's hushed voice. "I followed her down to the lakefront, because she was so upset. She was laying on the rocks when I found her."

The other voice was deep and serious, "So, you think it was an accident?"

"Yeah, she's just under a lot of pressure about her grades, and then there's a bunch of family stuff going on. I think Joanna was trying to run away from it all."

"Okay. Good to know. I'll talk to her when she wakes up. In the meantime, we'll keep monitoring her temperature. Can you give me her parents' phone number?"

Joanna wanted to yell out, *No! Don't call Mom!* but she didn't have the strength to form the words, let alone bring voice to them. Her eyelids fluttered as she squinted at the bright lights overhead while an odd sound croaked from the depths of her throat. She fought to stay awake but drifted back to sleep. She slipped into a dream where she was laying naked in a snowdrift that suddenly gave way, and she slid down a long slope. She tried to find something to grab in order to stop herself, but the slope was nothing but snow.

Still groggy, she felt blankets being repositioned over her shivering body. A quick flash of light in each eye made her squint again as she heard, "Welcome back. I'm Dr. Price."

"What happened?" Joanna asked in a raspy voice.

"You have a bit of hypothermia from that dip you took in the lake and a pretty good gash on your forehead. Isn't it a little early for the Polar Bear Plunge?" He chuckled at his own joke. "I thought that was a New Year's Day thing."

"I was in the lake? I remember walking down there, but not being in the water."

"Well, you were found laying on the rocks down on the lakefront. When you got here, your temperature was well below normal. We've been warming you up for the past 24 hours, and the good news is that we got you back to 98.6. We're still watching your fingers for signs of frostbite." Dr. Price held Joanna's hands, scanning them with trained eyes.

"Freaky. I don't remember any of that."

"It's not unusual to have some memory loss around a trauma. Your roommate was the hero for finding you before it was too late."

"Oh yeah! I do remember hearing Deborah …sometime after… where is she?"

"I don't know." He started to leave the room, then turned back. "Oh, is there anything that's bothering you?"

"Bothering me? No. Well, I'm a little stressed out, but I'm a college student."

"Well, I'll get you some contact information for the mental health services on campus," he said turning to leave again, then added, "And, you really should try to stop that nail-biting habit."

Joanna rested fitfully in her hospital bed, drifting in and out of sleep, but in her semi-conscious state, she was aware of her parents sitting at her bedside.

"Really, Peter, can't you even bother to put on a clean shirt when you come out in public? You've got paint on your collar."

"Well, it's not like I had any advanced notice or anything, you know," Peter countered defensively.

Joanna heard her mother sigh heavily, then take a deep breath and offer another unsolicited opinion, "And Peter, if it's not too much trouble, you might consider using those nose hair clippers my mother gave you last Christmas."

Come on, Dad, don't let her treat you like that, Joanna thought as she heard Peter draw in a breath. But, the buzzing of Beverly's phone squelched any response Peter might have made.

"Oh, Millie, it was awful," Joanna heard her mother moan. "Mr. Thompson is the most difficult client I've ever worked with. He's some New York City corporate hotshot whose company is relocating him out here – to the 'hinterland' as he calls it."

Beverly sighed. "Oh, I have such a migraine tonight." In the haze of her peripheral vision, Joanna perceived her mother sitting in the easy chair next to the hospital bed, massaging her temples; Joanna's father leaned against the doorframe as if he needed a quick exit.

"Do you know, I picked up Mr. NYC on time this morning from O'Hare," Beverly went on. "On time...showed him four houses and two townhomes, managed to squeeze in a nice, relaxing lunch, and get him back to the airport in time for his flight home—all this in Chicago rush hour and construction traffic mind you. And, all I got from him was, 'Well, I'll talk to my wife about what we saw today, but I'm sure I'll have to come back out here for another day of viewing. It will take some effort, but I'll see if my company will pay for another trip.'"

Joanna rolled her eyes, *It's all about you, isn't it Mom?*

"Then, if that's not bad enough, I'm sitting on the Kennedy, and my cell phone goes off. I'm thinking, 'Oh no, it's Mr.

Thompson calling from the Airport Club.' Thank goodness it wasn't, but that call really had me upset. Guess who it was?"

Assuming the call was about her current situation, Joanna smiled to herself at her mother's concern for her. *Aw, Mom you really do care about me.*

"No Millie, it was worse than that. It was Teddy. Mom's having some pain in her right knee after her run-in with that damn dog and what should he do about it? I just cannot believe how someone his age can be so immature. Now I have another mess to clean up."

As Beverly paused at some comment Millie was making on the other end of the call, Joanna's spirits fell. *I should have known. It **really is** always about you, isn't it Mom?*

Peter muttered under his breath with thinly veiled contempt, "Things in this family would fall apart if you didn't hold it all together for us."

Seemingly unaware of Peter's comment, Beverly continued, "You would think Teddy could figure some of this out for himself. But it is Teddy we're talking about. Anyway, I told him I'd look up Mom's insurance information when I got home, and wouldn't you know, no sooner had I hung up than my phone went off again. It was just so awful. I answered the call, and it was a doctor calling about Joanna. Oh, Millie, I don't know what I'd do if…" Beverly paused. "Millie, are you still there? Damn dropped call," she muttered to herself."

Is Mom actually getting emotional about me? Joanna's eyelids fluttered as she attempted to make sense of things. *What time is it?* Realizing she had no answer, she wondered, *What **day** is it?* Confused, she opened her eyes. "Mom? Dad? Why are you here? Together?"

"Why are we here?" Joanna's mother repeated. "Because obviously you need us."

"There are ways of asking for help other than jumping in the lake, Pumpkin," said Joanna's father.

"Peter, don't make jokes." Joanna's mother stood, straightened her skirt, and walked over to the bed. Stroking Joanna's hair more to straighten it than to comfort her, Beverly asked, "How are you feeling?"

Suppressing a shiver and painfully aware of the throb in her head, Joanna said, "I'm fine. The doctor said I could go back to school."

"Sure you can…" Peter started, and then stopped mid-sentence as Joanna noticed Beverly throw a frowning glare in Peter's direction.

"Well," Peter continued, "We'll stop by your dorm room and help you pack up your things, and then Mom will drive you back to the house."

Joanna felt a tightening in her stomach. "I have classes tomorrow. I can't go home."

Beverly's phone buzzed again, prompting her to scan its screen. Letting out a huff of air, she groaned, "It's Teddy. What now?" Poking at her phone, she muttered, "Why can't I ever get a signal in this room?" as she exited.

Joanna felt more relaxed with her mother outside the area for the moment. She seized the opportunity and turned to her dad for support. "Dad, you know I'm fine. I'll get behind if I take a break."

Peter leaned over and kissed her forehead. "You're right, kiddo, you will be fine. But you know what, we'll work that out later. Let's take it one step at a time. We'll get you home, we'll get situated, then we'll talk."

The words "what do we need to talk about" were about to roll out of Joanna's mouth.

Beverly burst back into the room. "I can't believe it." Her complexion was pale, and her eyes were wide. "Mother's injured, and this time she's in the hospital."

Joanna gasped.

Peter asked, "What is it? What happened?"

"Apparently she fell again. It's too soon to tell what all the damage is, but hopefully we'll know when we get the x-ray results."

Peter asked with a grimace, "Was it Peanut?"

"I couldn't get all the details out of Teddy, but he assured me it wasn't because of the dog."

"And you trust him?" asked Peter.

"Definitely not, but what choice do I have," came Beverly's sharp reply. She hung her head in one hand and massaged her forehead.

Joanna thought, *Well Mom, if Mr. Thompson wasn't so important to you, you could go out there and take care of Grandma yourself.*

Just then the nurse stepped in with Joanna's discharge papers. "Transport will be here with a wheelchair soon, and then we'll get you out of here and on your way."

Joanna took the papers and scanned through them. The one that directed her to the campus counseling service caught her eye. Maybe the doctor was right. *Being in this family is making me feel crazy.*

Beverly let out another heavy sigh. "I can't believe all of this happened in the same day! I just hope I don't get another angry house hunting call from Mr. Thompson. That would just be the icing on the cake."

"Wow, Mom," Joanna said. "You make it sound like I fell in the lake just to give you a hard time. Sorry for the inconvenience."

"Don't be silly, Joanna"

"You always say silly, Mom, but don't you really want to say stupid?"

Peter interjected, "Whoa, whoa! Settle down, Joanna. You've had a really tough day."

Joanna took a deep breath, but still felt anger rising in her chest.

Beverly sighed again. "Look, Joanna, I'm sorry it sounded like that to you, but I don't have time for any of this right now. Grandma nearly killed herself, she lives five states away, and she has an idiot for a son who is supposed to be her caregiver. But he can't even take care of himself, let alone her. If I don't step in and make some decisions, who knows what will happen?"

Joanna shot back, "Maybe I should go to live with Grandma. That would be easier for everybody."

"Are you going to go live with her in the nursing home, because that's where she's headed!"

Caught in her mother's withering stare, Joanna felt a wave of queasiness pass through her midsection. The idea of her mother shuttling her Grandma off to an old farts' home conjured up memories of her summer volunteer work at Sunny Hill. Imagining her grandmother in that environment of vacant stares, rancid smells, and debilitating loneliness made her feel physically ill. *But what can I do to keep a move from happening if Madame Beverly has decided it will be so?*

Chapter 6

Joanna was relieved to be back in her dorm room after a night at home with her mother. Curled up on her bed, hugging her pillow to her chest, she finally felt warm again. Her dorm was always unbearably hot, but today it felt just right.

Joanna imagined that for most people, recuperation at home involved hot tea and breakfast in bed. *Ah, but no room service for me! I can't remember Mom ever doing that.* Shaking her head and smiling to herself, Joanna thought. *Why am I not surprised? Mom never was the warm and fuzzy type. All the warmth mom could have showered on me went to her clients and the next big sale.* Perplexed but not surprised by her mother's maternal modus operandi, Joanna shrugged and shifted her focus.

Surveying the piles of clothes and books that made up most of her college life, she pulled her suitcase out of the closet, laid it on the bed, then absent-mindedly placed a pile of sweaters next to the suitcase. While she was at home being ignored, Joanna had formulated a plan. It was the first thing she had felt sure about in a long time. But in order for her plan to work, she needed her father's help. Grabbing her phone, she sent him a quick text and then thought, *Yikes, I hope this works.*

Joanna stared back at the empty suitcase and strategized which books to pack and which ones to leave behind. Unable to decide, she opened her calculus book. *If I can finish this assignment, I can leave this book here.* After a half an hour of futile attempts at solving a particularly vexing integral, she went back to packing.

The click of the door caught her attention, followed by Deborah's cheery greeting, "Hey Chickie! Welcome back!"

"Thanks," Joanna said distractedly.

"Are you packing already?" Deborah pointed to the suitcase on the bed. "It's not Thanksgiving break yet."

"I'm just leaving a couple of days early." Joanna pulled several t-shirts out of a drawer.

"Where are you going? You're not running away are you?" asked Deborah. "You know most young female runaways get caught in human trafficking and end up in the sex trade."

Joanna stopped packing and glared at Deborah, whose eyes twinkled. A smile crept over Joanna's face. "You're messing with me, aren't you?"

Deborah put on a sober expression as best she could, "I just thought you should consider that before you bolt."

Joanna stared back at Deborah. "What? What are you talking about? I'm not running away." Joanna rolled her eyes. "And I'm certainly not becoming a prostitute!"

"Just make sure you come back," said Deborah as she crammed her Econ textbook into her backpack. She started to leave the room, but turned back, "Joanna, you have a male visitor."

Peter appeared in the doorway, gave Joanna a quick kiss on the cheek and said, "Hey Pumpkin, I got your text."

Joanna squirmed away. "Wow, you got here fast."

"Well, you know I'm not that far away, now that I have my own place."

She sat down and patted the bed beside her.

Peter sat down. "Is everything okay? Looks like you're packing. You know we're not flying to Nana Jackman's until Wednesday."

"Dad, I know you and Nana are expecting me for Thanksgiving, but when we land in New Jersey, I have to go to Grandma Ruth's," Joanna blurted out.

"Now wait a minute. Your mother and I had an agreement. She can't just change the plan to suit her whims!"

"It's okay, Dad..."

"No! I am not going to stand for this. I spent too many years putting up with that shit."

"I'm not going with Mom. I'm going on my own."

"What do mean?"

"I want to go to Grandma's house and stay for a few days, 'cause I think I can make her house safer for her."

Peter took off his glasses and rubbed them on his shirt. "But, what about Thanksgiving with Nana and me?" he frowned.

"I know. I'm sorry, Dad." She put her head on his shoulder. "I was looking forward to it, but somebody needs to stick up for Grandma before it's too late."

"Too late?"

"I just want a chance to help Grandma before Mom takes everything away from her." Joanna paused, giving him a meaningful look. "And, you know what that's like, don't you?"

Peter sighed in defeat. "Yeah, I do."

"You know how much I like spending time with you, but Grandma really needs me right now."

"Okay, I guess I can see that, but what's your mother going to say about this?"

"That's the beauty of it. Mom will think I'm at school and then with you. I'll take care of everything before Mom realizes I'm gone. But I do need one thing from you, Dad. Could you take me to the airport?"

Chapter 7

The flight to New Jersey was a quick two-hour trip. The taxi ride from Newark Airport to the small town of Neshanic Station was only 45 minutes, but seemed slow as Joanna contemplated her decision to "visit" her grandmother. Joanna gazed out the window from the backseat of the car as she rode through the neighborhood where Grandma Ruth lived. She loved the way the trees arched gracefully over the streets. Even without leaves, they were beautiful. As the cab turned onto Olive Lane, Joanna smiled at the thought of seeing Ruth. She closed her eyes, imagining the refreshing shade of the maple trees during summertime visits, remembering her last trip to Neshanic Station just before high school started. *Six years ago? Has it really been that long?*

The taxi slowed to a stop in front of a small, sad-looking house. "644 Olive Lane. There you go, Miss," said the driver.

She slid out of the taxi and retrieved her suitcase from the trunk without the driver's help. "Thanks," she mumbled as she tipped him with the change in her pocket.

Joanna paused, taking in the character of the old house. The brown, shingle-style facade was peeling with age. A picture window, the largest feature on the front of the house, was cloudy in one corner and partly obscured by the over-grown juniper bushes. A fiberglass awning shaded the window from above.

Her eye followed the cement walkway, cracked and uneven, up to the front step that was framed by a rusty metal railing on one side. The driveway, two tracks of cement wide enough for the tires of a car, led to a one-car garage. Joanna cocked her head to one side; the garage appeared to be tilting away from the house. It had all seemed so quaint when Joanna was younger, but now it seemed worn and tired.

Joanna's phone buzzed, jarring her thoughts. She reached into her pocket. A text from Deborah: "Where r u"

"New Jersey." Joanna aimed her camera at the house, snapped a picture and sent it off. "Gmas."

"Huh?" came the reply.

"Here to help. Gma fell again. Ttyl."

Tucking her phone back into her pocket, Joanna took a step toward the house, attempting to wheel her suitcase up the walkway. Instead of following along smoothly behind her, its wheels caught in a large crack, refusing to move. She gave her bag a violent jerk, dislodging it from the crevice, and proceeded to drag it along behind her. Lifting her suitcase, she climbed up the three crumbling front steps and then knocked gently on the aluminum screen door. After a brief wait and no answer, she opened the screen door and tried the knob of the main door. It was open. Her heart fluttered in anticipation. She slowly swung it open and called, "Hello?"

"Who's there?" came a muffled and somewhat feeble reply. Her grandmother's voice—hearing it here in the old house made Joanna feel as though she had just been outside playing in the yard and was being called in for supper.

"Hello! It's me, Joanna." She cautiously stepped into the tiny and cramped living room. It was hard to see anything at all from the doorway. The bushes and awning obstructed the window on the outside, and the heavy drapes covered the inside, making the living room remarkably dark even though the front of the house faced south. Squinting into the room, her eyes swept back and forth, looking for any sign of life in the dimly lit space. Joanna focused in on the plastic floor runner, partially seen and partially remembered, that led from the front door, across the avocado-green shag carpet, through the living room to the kitchen. Another plastic path connected the front door to the bedroom hallway. As Joanna's eyes adjusted to the muted tones in the room, she parked her suitcase and smiled at being in her grandmother's presence.

"Hi, Grandma!"

"Oh, well goodness gracious! What a pleasant surprise!"

Joanna smiled and crossed the room.

"Land sakes! What are you doing here, Joanna?" asked Ruth.

"Well, you know, after our Skype, I thought I'd come and visit you for Thanksgiving," Joanna stretched the truth.

"Well, lean down here and give me a hug. I'd get up, sweetie, but this bum foot of mine keeps me from getting around too well right now." Ruth pointed to the hard, plastic boot on her injured foot.

Joanna bent over and looped her arms around her grandmother's neck. Stooping down to that level was tricky, especially in the heels and skirt she was wearing. *Well, this is awkward! I'm not sure why I picked this outfit. I guess I was trying to impress Grandma. What a silly idea!* Joanna thought.

Joanna went for the quick pat-on-the-back type hug, but as soon as she was within reach, her grandmother latched onto her with the strength of a high school bantamweight wrestler. The grip was physically powerful, and she didn't seem at all eager to let go. Joanna patted at her grandmother's shoulder with one hand, while reaching to hold onto the back hem of her skirt with the other in an effort to cover her upward-flung fanny.

By the time she was released from her grandmother's clasp, Joanna's eyes had fully adjusted to her surroundings, and she got a good look at her grandma: glasses hanging crookedly on her face as she beamed up over the thick lenses at Joanna, the apple of her eye.

"Oh, sweetie, it's so good to have you here." Ruth reached over, took Joanna's hand, and began petting it. Smiling back at her, Joanna tried in vain to gain a comfortable stance in the half bent-over position into which she had been pulled, all the while trying to balance on her less than sensible choice of shoes.

"Is it okay if I turn on a light?" Joanna asked.

"Sure, sweetie."

Joanna's eyes passed over the room again, searching for a light. Squeezing past another recliner in the over-furnished room, Joanna switched on a palm-tree shaped lamp on the end table next to the plaid couch. "That's better, Grandma." Joanna squished back through the furniture. The lamp shed a soft glow over the empty recliner, highlighting its duct-taped patches. "Is this Gramp's chair? It seems a lot more worn out than I remember from when I was here for his funeral." Joanna turned to sit in the old chair.

"Oh no. Don't sit there. Pull up a seat and sit with me, dear." Ruth grabbed Joanna's hand and guided her to sit on the footstool by her chair.

Joanna stepped toward the ottoman which was in the same, sadly-worn shape as her grandpa's weathered Lazy-Boy and sat down, trying to avoid the sticky duct tape streak that ran across the center of the seat. Unlatching her hand from her grandmother's grip, Joanna sighed and ran a hand through her long brown hair.

"Do you have a headache, Sweetie?" Ruth asked with love and a bit of concern.

"No, not really—just a little tired from all my travel today.

Sitting up straight and closing her eyes, Joanna slowly rolled her head around in a circle as she gently rubbed at her temples.

No sooner had her eyes closed when Joanna felt the ottoman take a 90 degree spin, and then a pair of hands were upon her shoulders, massaging them with a strength unusual for someone her grandmother's age.

"Wow, Grandma, if you were able to walk, I bet you could wrestle me to the floor and march across my back like some chiropractor gone wild."

"You know, I used to give your grandpa a mean massage," she recalled as she shoved up her sleeves and continued kneading Joanna's neck. "He'd come home from his job all wound up, tight as a spring, head throbbing, back aching. It just became a routine for us - him relating the happenings of his day, while I rubbed and squeezed the stress right out of him." She went into a karate-chopping motion across Joanna's upper back and then commenced to rub gently at her temples in a small circular motion.

Wallowing in post-massage relaxation, Joanna failed to immediately notice the change in her grandma's grip. Opening her eyes, she spun around and saw Ruth rocking front to back in her chair, trying to build up enough momentum to stand. Realizing what was happening before Ruth could rise, Joanna exclaimed "Hey now, Grandma! Don't you think you need to settle back down into your chair?"

"Oh, I'm fine, dear. I just thought you'd like a nice cup of tea."

Joanna held out her hand and protested. "I'm here to see you, not be waited on by you. You stay right there. I'll get the tea." Then rising, Joanna proceeded down the plastic runway and toward the kitchen.

Standing in the doorway, Joanna smiled, "Just like I remember." Then giving the harvest gold kitchen a closer look, she thought, *only a little more faded.* Focusing again on the task at hand, she filled the teakettle and put it on the stove.

"Grandma, I always liked spending time in the kitchen with you," Joanna called into the living room as she slid the glass cabinet door open and carefully removed a china teacup from the heavily bowed shelf. She fingered a chip on its rim. *Huh. Broken, just like me,* she thought as she returned the cup, saying, "You're not good enough." Selecting another cup, she inspected it. "That's better, you're good enough." Finding another acceptable vessel, she carried both to the table. She retrieved the kettle, and as she poured hot water into her grandmother's cup, she was distracted by a squeaking sound followed by a low groan.

"How's that tea coming, Sweetie?" Ruth asked, seating herself at the table.

"Grandma, you shouldn't be up and about, should you?"

"Oh, I'm fine, dear. This looks lovely. How about some of those cookies in the cabinet?"

"Oh, yeah. Sorry. I meant to get those. I'm just kind of distracted." Joanna let out a long, sad sigh.

"Is something the matter, dear?"

For an instant, Joanna wanted to share everything with her grandma like she would have when she was ten years old, but she wasn't sure how to start and didn't have the energy to organize her thoughts.

"No. I'm fine, Grandma," Joanna lied. "How are you?"

"Well, I've been better, but I'm still alive, God-willing. You know how it is to be 79."

"Grandma! You know I'm only 20."

"Ah, to be young again. Remind me how that is."

Challenging…disjointed…sucky…. She frowned down at the scuffed linoleum floor. *Life seemed so much simpler when I was a kid.*

"It's not quite what I expected."

"Oh? How so?" asked Ruth as she sipped her tea.

"I don't know. I'm just kind of tired."

"A little tea will fix you right up!"

After savoring her tea, Joanna stood and carried her cup to the sink. "I think I'll go check out my room."

"Well," Ruth hesitated. "I think we'll have to move a few things before you can go to bed."

"That's okay. I'll go have a look." The thought of seeing the bedroom she had called home during the summer she turned ten was suddenly exciting to Joanna. It was so old and charming with its four-poster bed and lace curtains.

"Certainly. I'll come with you." Ruth moved herself to the edge of her chair and swayed back and forth a couple of times before she stood. Even with the amount of effort it took for her to rise, Joanna was impressed by her grandmother's mobility. Grasping her walker, Ruth hobbled along on her good foot down the short hallway to the spare bedroom. Joanna followed and reached around the corner to turn on the light which illuminated a jumble of boxes and piles of old clothing. She let out a gasp.

The four-poster bed was piled high with books and clothes, and the pathway into the room was barely wide enough for even a tiny person like her grandmother to navigate. Baffled, Joanna asked, "Where will we put all of these things?"

Joanna remembered that her grandma liked to save things. Ten years ago, when Joanna stayed the summer, there were some things piled around the house, but the piles seemed as if they had been breeding in a prolific way since Joanna had last stayed in the guest bedroom.

From her vantage point in the hallway, Ruth said, "There might be some room in the closet," prompting Joanna to squeeze into the room and attempt to reach the closet door. The boxes were stacked waist high, and she nearly sprawled over the top of one after she tripped on something immovable in her path. When she reached the closet, a sigh of relief escaped her lips as she realized that the doors slid on a track and didn't open into the packed room. But as Joanna pushed the door to one side, she groaned; the closet was filled from floor to ceiling with more boxes.

"Uh…I don't think there's any room in the closet," Joanna said. She wanted to sit down and cry, but there was nowhere to sit. Instead she sucked in a deep breath and said, "I'll start clearing off the bed."

"Okay, dear," Ruth answered. "I'll be right back. Tea always goes right through me, don't you know." She hobbled out of the bedroom, her walker creaking along the way.

Threading her way back through the cardboard maze toward the bed, Joanna contemplated a desire to run straight out of the house. Rubbing her eyes, she stifled her urge to flee in favor of helping Grandma. "Better get started," she muttered to herself as she stared at the collection of possessions that filled the bedroom. She stretched and yawned, wondering where to begin.

A yellow Whitman's Candy Sampler box caught her eye. The top was faded, but the cardboard was sturdy, safely protecting its contents. Curious about what was inside, Joanna slipped the lid off – not sure what to expect, but not at all expecting what was inside. A horde of prickly, gray hair-rollers – the kind that stay in place without the use of a clip or hairpin – clung together in their candy-box vault. Joanna furled her brow and thought, *why would anyone be saving these things?* She reached for one of the curlers, but they came out in one substantial clump. Suspending the rollers squeamishly between two fingers, Joanna noted that they were intertwined with hair and flecked with dandruff. *Grandma doesn't still use these, does she?* she wondered. But, before she had time to think it through, she frowned and sniffed the air. "What is that smell?" She dropped the curlers and fanned the air as the overwhelming odor of mold and dirty hair wafted toward her nose. "That's disgusting!"

Feeling giddy with exhaustion, Joanna started to laugh as she considered possible reasons for saving these dirty curlers. *Maybe Grandma forgot she had them. Maybe that's Mom's hair. Maybe they could be used as a giant scrubber for floor stains. Maybe she used them to brush the dog.* In the midst of her pondering, Joanna failed to hear Ruth come into the room.

"Hello, dear. I'm back." Ruth smiled from the doorway as she noticed the wad of rollers. "Would you like me to set your hair?"

"What? Oh, no," stammered Joanna, as she grabbed the rollers back. "Just starting to put your things away." She smiled, trying not to look too disgusted, as she stowed the rollers back in their candy box.

"Well, if you ever need a new hairstyle, dear, you just let me know." Ruth said. "Don't you know, I used to be in high demand by the ladies in my neighborhood. They would pay me 50 cents for setting their hair and another 10 cents for a bit of spray. Made some of my best friends talking to the backs of their heads, while I worked my magic." Ruth closed her eyes and smiled, obviously pleased with the memory coming into focus in her mind.

"Oh, were you a hair dresser?" asked Joanna politely, trying not to grimace as she imagined the poor woman whose hair was mercilessly plucked from her scalp as the rollers were pulled from her tresses.

"Oh, no, dear, I just had a knack for beauty aids, I guess." Ruth paused, "Well that, and the fact that I was the only gal in my area who would do a set so cheaply."

Flabbergasted, Joanna searched for something to say. She wanted to say, *I wouldn't be caught dead in those things*, but she refrained and said instead, "Do you still use them on your friends?"

"Oh, no, dear. I didn't even know I had those old things," Ruth smiled. "They'd need a good cleaning before I could use them again, and they do kind of smell bad. Don't think I've used those since the 1960's. Besides, those girls down at the beauty parlor do such a nice job now-a-days."

Joanna found herself enjoying the story of the curlers even in her annoyance at the mess. "Okay then, I'll just throw these away." *One box down…* she thought as she realized getting rid of this one small box wasn't going to put a dent in the work ahead of her.

"Oh no! Don't throw them away," Ruth exclaimed protectively. "Those curlers have a lot of good memories in them, and I might need them again someday."

"Ohhh-kay. But, I need to make room to sleep. Where do you want me to put this stuff?"

"Well…you can just stack some of those things next to the piano in the living room…for now." Yawning, Joanna scooped up the closest container as she ushered Ruth out of the bedroom and into her chair in the living room. After multiple trips to and from the bedroom, Joanna sat on the edge of the bed and surveyed the mishmash of disorganization. "Guess there's no need to hit the gym this week, but at least I have a place to sleep." Exhausted, but satisfied, she headed to the living room where she found Ruth sitting in the dark, glued to the TV.

"What's up pussycat?" asked Ruth as Joanna flung herself into Gramps' chair.

"I'm so tired…and it's only 7:30?" Joanna was stunned as she checked her watch. It had been a long day. "Guess I'll turn in, Grandma," Joanna yawned, heading toward the bedroom.

She squeezed through the maze of remaining boxes and flopped down on the bed. Instantly, a poof of dust rose from the old quilt, engulfing her. Wheezing and coughing, she pulled herself up, trying to catch her breath. "Well, that figures," Joanna balled up the quilt and kicked it to the foot of the bed. Snuggling down under the covers, she made herself comfortable…but sleeping was another matter. Her thoughts spun in irreconcilable loops just like they had when she last tried to run away from her problems back on campus.

Chapter 8

Shoulders aching, Joanna gazed out at the mountains of boxes surrounding her bed. A sliver of light squeezed past the shades, telling her at least it was after sunrise. Reaching for her phone, she winced in pain, "Ow!" and then "Damn!" as she realized that she had forgotten to plug it in. Extricating herself from the room, Joanna massaged her neck and shuffled off toward the kitchen, hair disheveled, eyelids barely open.

Finding Ruth in the kitchen, Joanna queried, "How long have you been up, Grandma?"

"Since 5:00." Ruth, fully dressed, sat at the kitchen table holding a cup of tea.

As she leaned back against the kitchen counter, Joanna stretched and yawned. "What time is it now?" she asked.

"Well, it's already 8:30. This is my mid-morning break, don't you know."

Joanna glanced at the kitchen clock. *Well, I guess if you get up at 5:00, 8:30 is mid-morning.* Shaking her head to force the fog from her brain, she asked, "Grandma, what have you been up to this morning?"

"Oh, I don't know. A little bit of this and little bit of that." Ruth rocked herself upright and hobbled toward Joanna, but before Joanna could react, Ruth reached past her and popped a slice of raisin bread into the toaster. "Oh dear," she winced.

Joanna perked up. "What's wrong, Grandma. Are you ok?"

"Oh, I'm fine," Ruth replied.

Joanna gently guided her grandmother back to a chair at the kitchen table.

Ruth held her side and took a shallow breath. "Every time I think these old ribs are getting better, that same old pain sneaks up on me again. Dad gum it! I sure am ready to get back to my normal self."

"Your ribs? I thought it was your foot."

"Well, when I hurt my foot, I also bruised my ribs on one side."

Retracing her steps, Joanna retrieved the slice of raisin toast. As she headed back to the table, Joanna looked directly at Ruth and raised her eyebrows, "And, just how is it that you happened to injure yourself?"

"Well, I fell," answered Ruth vaguely as she reached for the honey.

"Yes, that's what Mom said. But, *how* did you fall? What were you doing?"

"Oh, I was helping the neighbors, dear. Morgan, she's six, and Nathan, he's eight. Those two are the sweetest little neighbors I could ask for. So polite. Always waving and bringing me little treats. Why for Valentine's Day this year, those two left a beautiful handmade card at my back door. Where is that? I think it's in this pile here." Ruth shuffled through the mound of papers on the teacart adjacent to the kitchen table.

"Grandma, are you sure it would still be there? Valentine's Day was nine months ago."

"Here it is!" Ruth said as she pulled out a red heart-shaped piece of paper.

Joanna rolled her eyes. *Of course, it is. What was I thinking! You have fifty years of your crap stuffed in the back bedroom.* "What does this have to do with your fall?" Joanna tried to redirect the conversation.

But, Ruth ignored her and read:

"Roses are red,
Violets are blue,
Dear Mrs. Lathrop,
We really love you!"

"They sound nice," Joanna replied – more out of politeness than interest. "But, just how did you fall?"

Silence filled the room as sunlight streamed in through the window. Seemingly deep in thought, Ruth gazed off into a corner of the kitchen, her eyes fixed on nothing. Joanna watched for a moment then rose from her chair to retrieve the teakettle from the stove.

Ruth broke her far-off gaze and said, "Did I ever tell you that I was the pogo stick champion of my whole school when I was in the fourth grade?"

"No, you didn't, Grandma, but how is that related to your fall?"

Undeterred by Joanna's inquiry, Ruth continued, "Well, I was, I'm proud to tell you. It was just after the Christmas break that year, and the weather was exceptionally balmy for January. Raymond Micelli brought his brand new pogo stick to school that day."

Well, she's obviously avoiding the question. Guess I'll just let her talk. Joanna nodded her head as she straightened the pile of papers from which the neighbor kids' valentine card had been pulled.

"Raymond was a shy boy, even more shy than me, but when he got on that stick and started jumping, there was no stopping him. At first, he stayed over in the corner of the schoolyard, out of sight and away from the popular students. But, as he continued to hop without stopping, more and more of our classmates gathered around him and counted along with each jump '116, 117, 118…' As he was nearing 200, I guess the crowd got to be too much for him. He misstepped and ended his astounding pogo stick pounce at 199.

"Everyone was in awe of Raymond's ability. He didn't say much, but you could tell he was proud of himself. Other students wanted to try, but when Patrick Hanson stepped up, the others backed away. Patrick was a big boy, and he was the captain of our eighth grade basketball team. If anyone could beat Raymond's record, we all knew it would be Patrick."

Ruth smiled, shook her head at the memory, and took a sip of tea.

"Uh, huh," Joanna was only half-listening, as she shuffled through expired coupons, outdated reminder cards from the dentist, a stained menu from a Chinese restaurant, a broken earring, a half-finished crossword puzzle, and a church bulletin from…June. And, those were just the things on the top. *Wow!* To Joanna the randomness of what Ruth considered worth saving was just as interesting as Ruth's detailed musings.

Continuing her story, Ruth said, "Well, Patrick grabbed Raymond's pogo stick and leapt up onto it, but after only three jumps, Patrick and the pogo stick pitched sideways. The stick landed on its side with a crash as Patrick managed to jump out of its way. Some of the other students tried the pogo stick but without much success, and finally the group started to drift away. No one had come anywhere close to Raymond's 199-jump record.

"When my brother, Melvin, said he'd try, the remaining kids laughed at the notion. Melvin was in the third grade, short, and wiry, and he turned blue at the slightest chill in the air. No one thought he could lift the pogo stick, let alone leap up onto it. But, what everyone didn't know was that we had a pogo stick at our house, and Melvin and I practiced on it all the time. To everyone's surprise, Melvin jumped near about 130 times before he fell off."

"Way to go Uncle Melvin!" Joanna commented. Rising from the table, thinking that the story had come to its conclusion, Joanna started scooping up a pile of newspapers to take to the recycling bin.

"Well, don't you know, your great Uncle Melvin has always been one to…" Ruth broke off suddenly. "Don't recycle those. I haven't done the puzzles yet. I got a little behind while I was laid up last week, don't you know."

"O-kay."

Without missing a beat, Ruth resumed her story, "Oh, Melvin was good, but I was even better, although much too shy to boast about it. Then, all of the sudden I heard Melvin say, 'If you think that was good, Ruth is even better. Here, Ruthie,' he said as he foisted the stick upon me."

Only half listening, Joanna continued her efforts to straighten the items on Ruth's kitchen table. In the process, she noticed Ruth's date book, which was open to the day's page and saw, "Doctor Killian, 9:15 a.m." Joanna interrupted. "Excuse me, Grandma, but do you have a doctor's appointment this morning?"

"What does the calendar say, dear?"

"Doctor Killian, 9:15 am." Joanna glanced at the clock. It was 8:45. "Where is the doctor's office?" her voice rising in urgency.

"Oh, it's in a building over in Flemington. It'll only take about ten minutes to get there."

"But we have to get ready to go!" Joanna dashed out of the kitchen and to the shower.

Fifteen minutes later, with her hair still wet, Joanna helped Ruth to the car, and they sped off down Olive Lane.

Despite the abrupt beginning to their trip, Joanna was feeling happy about spending some quality time with her grandmother.

As they hummed along down 202 toward Flemington, Joanna steered back to her original inquiry. "So, now just how did you hurt yourself?"

"Hmm. Where was I?" Ruth paused. "Oh, yes, I was taken aback by Melvin's boast. I was very nervous that everyone was waiting, and the stick was in my hand, but I knew I could out jump Raymond. So, I jumped up onto it."

Joanna opened her mouth in an effort to redirect Ruth yet again, but then realizing the futility of her action, she smiled, deciding instead to enjoy her grandmother's reminiscences.

"I started slowly, then gaining height with every bounce, I easily reached 100, then 150. As I neared 200, the kids were all around, counting along with me. Normally, I didn't like being the center of attention, but if there was one thing I was good at, it was the pogo stick, so I kept on jumping. Land sakes, was that fun! 200 came easily, as did 250 and then 300. I was still going strong when the schoolmaster rang the bell, signaling the end of recess. I dismounted and was enthusiastically congratulated on my athletic expertise. Oh, it was a glorious feeling!" Ruth paused gazing out the car window as she basked in the glory of her past triumph. She let out a sigh. "Poor old Raymond never brought his pogo stick to school again. I felt kind of bad for him, but it was fun being the envy of all my classmates."

Joanna maneuvered the car into the lot and parked. "Grandma, that's really cool," said Joanna with a hint of pride. "Well, not the part about Raymond, but about you."

"Sometimes I still feel like I should be in the 4th grade. I don't know how I ended up in this wrinkly, old body." Ruth let out a slight groan as she tried to readjust herself in her seat.

"Oh, Grandma, you're not old."

Ruth smiled at Joanna and reached for her hand. "My little Joanna," Ruth beamed at her granddaughter. "I'm so glad you're here, Sweetie."

"Me too," Joanna replied, holding her grandmother's hand and feeling quite loved.

The building Ruth pointed out as the doctor's office looked under construction and abandoned, but Ruth insisted that her doctor had just moved to this new location. Joanna was skeptical, but after instructing Ruth to remain in the car, she agreed to try the door. The main entrance and all visible doors were locked. Joanna returned to the car perplexed. Ruth dug deep into her purse and handed Joanna the "We're Moving" flyer she had been given at her last appointment. Joanna studied the crumpled paper and found the date of the move was December 10th.

"Grandma, the flyer says the move is scheduled for December."

Ruth peered at the flyer, adjusting her glasses. "Oh, so it does" she said. "I didn't see that at all. They should have written it larger."

Joanna called the telephone number on the flyer, explained their predicament and drove, somewhat over the speed limit, to the correct office location.

Their arrival in the office was evident as Ruth banged her walker against almost every hard surface as she made her way to check in. Looking up from behind the glass, the office receptionist acknowledged their presence by reprimanding them on the "need for timeliness in one's arrival for a pre-planned appointment." Ruth and Joanna sat down in the waiting room, expecting a long wait for the now-past appointment. However, shortly, they were directed into the examination room where Joanna reviewed with Ruth the purpose of the visit.

"Well, let's see," Ruth pondered. "I've got this pain in my back," she said, describing all the positions that caused her pain. "Last time I was here, Dr. Killian asked if I had pain anywhere, and I didn't mention my back. What do you think? Should I tell him today?"

"Sure, might as well, since we're here," Joanna replied. "But, don't forget to talk about your foot and your ribs."

Just then the doctor's assistant, Peggy, walked in saying, "Hello, Mrs. Lathrop. How are we feeling today?"

"Well, I don't know about you, but I've had some trouble with my bowel movements. Constipation, don't you know. Dr. Janice started me on a stool softener and that did the trick. I had a lovely bowel movement this morning."

As Peggy listened intently, Joanna prompted Ruth to concentrate on her orthopedic issues. "What about the pain in your back, Grandma?"

"Oh, yes, dear. Thank you." Ruth smiled at Joanna then proceeded to tell Peggy all the motions that caused pain. "It pains me when I walk, if I sit too long and when I roll over in bed. You'd think it could leave me alone at night, at least."

Peggy made some notations in Ruth's chart, reached into a drawer, extracted two paper garments, and directed Ruth on how to use them. As Peggy turned to make another notation in Ruth's chart, Ruth began to disrobe. By the time Peggy was ready to make her exit from the tiny room, Ruth was nude save her socks and the boot on one foot.

Seeing her grandmother naked made Joanna feel awkward. Ruth seemed shorter than Joanna remembered and somehow smaller, like Ruth had shrunk. Her pearlescent skin was thin and covered with wrinkles and an occasional lump and bump. Her shoulders slumped forward as if they were fighting against a heavy load. From the look of her chest and belly, her shoulders weren't the only parts of Ruth that had succumbed to the persistent force of gravity. On her left side, the telltale bruises from her fall were evident. "Grandma, next time you can probably wait until the nurse leaves the room, before you get changed." Joanna suggested as she held up the paper robe and averted her eyes.

"Well, dear, at my age, everything takes a little bit longer. Just hate to waste the doctor's precious time waiting on me. Besides it's nothing he hasn't seen before."

Joanna wished she could say the same. The crepey skin hanging from Ruth's upper arms flapped as she slipped into the paper gown. With a bit of assistance from Joanna, Ruth draped herself and managed to sit at the end of the examination table before Dr. Killian entered the room.

Geez, I'm going to make some kind of great doctor. 'I'm not sure what's wrong with you Mrs. Jones. Put your clothes back on, and I'll take a look.'

Dr. Killian knocked on the door and entered. "Hello, Mrs. Lathrop. How's that foot feeling?"

"Better, but my back is hurting something fierce today."

Dr. Killian asked Ruth to lie back, then asked, "Does this hurt?" as he raised her left leg. "How does this feel?"

"Ooo! Sore."

"And this?

"Ouch! The same."

"I think you're sore from using the walker," was the doctor's assessment. "That's hard work, you know."

"You're telling me! I can't wait to get rid of that thing."

Dr. Killian took off the protective boot and inspected her foot. "If your x-rays come back looking good, you can put some weight on that foot which will give your back a break."

Peggy re-entered and escorted Ruth off for her x-ray, returning her in short time to the exam room where she left Ruth and Joanna waiting for Dr. Killian to bring the results.

"Grandma, I still don't know what you were doing when you fell."

Smoothing out her paper gown, Ruth replied, "I told you. I was helping my neighbors."

"Don't tell me your fall has something to do with a pogo stick," Joanna said jokingly. But, then as she peered over at Ruth, her face went from a smile to a frown. "Just what were you doing to help those two kids?"

"Well, a few weeks ago I was watching my next door neighbor children playing with their pogo stick, and watching their attempts made me remember that grand day in the 4th grade. The thing is — Morgan and Nathan couldn't seem to get the hang of it. As a matter of fact, they were horrible at it. Every time they jumped up on the pogo stick, they lost their balance. It was sad to see them continue to try, only being able to get in three or four jumps before they lost their balance. It reminded me of poor old Patrick back in grammar school. The longer they jumped and failed, the more I wanted to give them some pointers. So, over I went."

Joanna shook her head in both disbelief and amazement as she could see where her grandmother's story was headed.

"Oh, they are such sweetie pies, but they just aren't very athletic. I tried to tell them everything I knew about how to balance on a pogo stick, from keeping a straight posture to squeezing their knees tight up against the center column as they jumped. Nothing worked. They had both been so hopeful when I first appeared and offered my assistance, but with failure after failure, they began to doubt my ability." Ruth gave a cocky little shake to her head and continued. "Finally, I decided I'd have to show them. It had been years and years since I last tried my skill with a pogo stick, but I figured it was like riding a bike; it would all come back to me."

Joanna slowly shook her head from side to side in disbelief. She couldn't help but smile a little at the picture in her mind of her

79-year-old Grandma bouncing on a pogo stick. "Did it?" Joanna asked with a mixture of awe, amusement, and concern in her voice.

"It did!" Ruth said, sounding a little incredulous. "I held the pogo stick in front of me, cautiously putting my right foot up onto one pad, and then, readying myself for the off-balance leap that would get me up and jumping. I hurled myself off the ground with one foot and came down on the footpads with both feet. The pogo stick recoiled and gave off an earsplitting squeak as my knees bent and pitched me right up into the second jump. I was reliving my 4th grade triumph, and it was wonderful! Seven, eight, nine… Morgan and Nathan counted as I bounced along their driveway. It was glorious, and they were impressed!"

Just then Dr. Killian returned, and Ruth's storytelling abruptly stopped.

"Are you telling your granddaughter the pogo stick story?" Dr. Killian asked.

"Yes, but don't spoil it," Ruth replied.

"I think I know how it ends, Grandma," Joanna smiled.

"But, you have to hear her tell it." Dr. Killian brought up Ruth's x-ray on the monitor in the room and pointed to the bone in her foot. "Looks better. You can start to put some weight on that foot, which will take some of the burden off your back. But, take it easy."

"That's good news," said Ruth. "And, I can get rid of this old walker?!"

"Just keep it nearby and be careful with your balance. I'll see you back in two weeks." Dr. Killian left the room, and Joanna moved over to Ruth's side to help her dress.

"Okay. He's gone now. You can tell me the rest of the story."

"Where was I?"

"You just started jumping."

"Oh yes. Well, I was wondering how long I could keep jumping, and then, I was on the ground. I don't really know what happened, but there was a sharp pain in my side, and my foot was throbbing." Joanna held Ruth's dress so she could slip her arms in the sleeves one at a time.

Ruth continued with a sheepish grin on her face. "Morgan stayed with me and held my hand, while Nathan ran for his mother. I do remember the nice young men who loaded me onto the gurney and the ambulance ride to the hospital. But, I can't really say how I ended up on the ground. Morgan said I hit an oily spot on their driveway. Nathan thought I lost my balance. Maybe my foot slipped from the jumping, and that's how I lost my balance. I bet that's it! My foot gave out. Not me. Either way, my pride was wounded, and my body was in physical pain."

"As the doctor scolded me for my antics and told me how lucky it was that I had only ended up with a few cracked ribs and a fractured foot, I thought about the phone call I'd have to make to your mother."

Joanna nodded knowingly.

"I knew Beverly would not be very happy with me. And, she wasn't. When I was finally settled into my room for overnight observation, I called to tell her the news. 'Oh, Mom,' was all she could say. I pictured her shaking her head in dismay, as she began to lecture me on my limitations as a senior citizen.

"Ooooh, that term – 'senior citizen'. It always makes me cringe, and Beverly knows it. I swear she likes to say it on purpose, just to remind me how old I am. I don't feel like I'm 79, but I guess these old bones just aren't as spry as they used to be. Well, despite Beverly's scolding and my discomfort, it was worth it. There is nothing like propelling yourself up and down on a pogo stick."

"Just remember that every time your back hurts," said Joanna.

Chapter 9

Back at home, Ruth settled into her recliner with the daily crossword puzzle. Joanna headed to the back bedroom to get her books, hoping to put in some desperately needed study time. Her plan was to study at Grandpa's old mahogany desk, but it sat in the back corner of her bedroom, heaped with junk. Not really in the mood to study anyway, Joanna abandoned her books and attempted to widen the path through the room by shifting and re-piling the contents of the room like a mini earthquake, building the mountains higher and widening the valley. Coming across a pile of old magazines, she picked them up and started for the recycle bin in the kitchen.

On her way through the living room, Joanna painfully caught her little toe under Ruth's piano that inexplicably overhung the kitchen doorway by just a few inches, causing the magazines to slide out of her grasp onto the kitchen floor. Joanna curled her toes under in an effort to curb the intense throbbing in her foot as she blurted out a few expletives. *Why would she put a piece of furniture in the doorway?* Recollecting the magazines, she hobbled across the kitchen and dumped the magazines onto the blue recycle bin underneath the table.

Sitting down at the table, Joanna rubbed her tender toes with one hand as she absent-mindedly flipped through a stack of Ruth's mail that had accumulated on the table. *How can anyone have this much junk mail?* Baffled, she sorted through the bundle of letters, dropping the majority of them into the recycle bin.

The table looked much tidier when she finished, but Joanna felt a bit uncomfortable disposing of her grandmother's mail without her permission. It seemed like something her mother would do. Too often, Joanna had seen her mother make decisions for Ruth without any input from Ruth herself.

Once, when she overheard her mother canceling several of Ruth's magazine subscriptions, Joanna remembered asking, "Mom, how can you do that without even asking Grandma if it's ok?"

"Joanna, please. She can't possibly get through all of these in a month – no one could. And, they just end up piling up at her house which makes more work for me when I visit."

"But, you could at least ask her," Joanna persisted.

"I could. And, I have. Your grandmother has a lot of difficulty parting with material possessions that are sentimental to her. But, you know Grandma. Everything is sentimental to her. It's better for everyone if I just do this without her knowledge."

No matter what her mother's rationale, Joanna had felt that it was underhanded. However, after encountering Ruth's tendencies first-hand, Joanna was already sifting through and pitching Ruth's stuff without her knowledge. Feeling a bit dishonest, Joanna hoped that Ruth would never discover what she was doing.

Already this morning Joanna had discarded a massive pile of junk mail—several pieces from the same agency. *Really?* There were a number of bills, which Joanna "filed" on the kitchen table for Ruth. She quickly discarded some 'You-May-Have-Already-Won' type letters. But, one piece of mail caught her eye. It was a notice from a donation group that would *happily* pick up 'useful household items and clothing in good condition.' "Whoa! This one is worth keeping." She read further, 'All you have to do is give us a call and set your items on the curb. It's so easy!' *This is the perfect opportunity to unload some of Grandma's stuff. The challenge will be getting her to agree, but how can she argue with donating her things to a good cause? And then once she does, how will I get it all out of the house? Oh well! I'll figure that out later.*

Having conquered the kitchen clutter and with a renewed sense of purpose, Joanna made the call to the donation site then headed back to battle with the chaos on the bedroom front.

With each new container she lifted, Joanna was tempted not to open it and just label it for the donation pile, but knowing that Ruth had saved all these things, for whatever reason she might have had, Joanna prompted herself to at least take a peek inside each one. Lifting the lid of an old sturdy Xerox box, she discovered one of her favorite childhood games—Yahtzee.

Opening the game box, she discovered some of the score sheets she and Ruth had filled out the last time they played which, by the scribbles at the top of Joanna's score pad, appeared to have been when Joann was ten. She smiled as she remembered some of the childish good luck moves she had invented in attempting to roll an actual Yahtzee: whispering the number she needed across the top of the die rolling cup, crossing the fingers on her left hand, while crossing her heart with her right hand.

Joanna glanced at the narrow swath she had cut in the mess and let out a heavy sigh. It seemed as if miles lay between her and the old desk. More from nostalgia than exhaustion, she declared, "I'm done. Time to take a break from sorting and challenge Grandma to a Yahtzee rematch."

Well into their afternoon Yahtzee respite, the excitement of the game and the afternoon sun started to make Joanna feel a bit warm. "Would it be okay if I open the window a bit?"

"Sure, but you'll need the axe," Ruth said matter-of-factly.

"The axe?!"

"Yes, right there behind the front door. I use it to prop open the window, because the springs are broken, don't you know."

Joanna, relieved that her Grandmother was not suggesting that she break a window open like a firefighter, went to retrieve the axe but was distracted by some commotion at the back door. She heard a dog barking excitedly as someone rattled the doorknob. Ruth didn't seem to pay any attention to what was going on, or maybe she didn't hear anything, but Joanna's heart skipped a beat at the thought of someone breaking in. The incessant fumbling and cursing at the door convinced Joanna that the person outside was not very sneaky and probably wouldn't do them any harm. *But, at least I have an axe nearby!*

"Anyone here?" came a husky, breathless voice from the kitchen.

"We're in the living room," hollered Ruth.

More foot stomping followed and then slow but steady footsteps made their way toward the living room. The footsteps paused, then came the most repulsive hacking cough, followed by several attempts to clear the throat, and topped off by one more harsh hack. Joanna wondered in anticipation who in the world it could be, but before she had her answer, the dog, a young looking black lab, came bounding into the living room, wagging its tail and sniffing everything in sight.

"Oh, Peanut, you're still here!" said Joanna as the dog sniffed at her and drooled unceremoniously on her pant leg and the floor. "Can you sit and shake?"

Instantly, Peanut, still drooling, sat in front of Joanna and offered her his paw. But, before she could respond, he was up and flittering around the room. Suddenly, a pile of magazines fell from the coffee table to the floor, causing Peanut to let out a surprised yip.

Just then, the unsavory character appeared in the doorway between the kitchen and living room. It was Nutty Uncle Teddy. "Peanut, sit. Stay," he wheezed. But instead, Peanut lunged toward Teddy and planted a long wet lick across his sweaty face. Teddy stood panting like he'd just run a marathon. He looked 20 years older than his actual age of 45, wore a Tommy Bahama button down shirt and Bermuda shorts, a rather stylish outfit except for the knee high, compression socks, orthopedic shoes and braces on each knee—and the fact that it was November.

Ruth was just completing a third roll for her two's and was forced to put a zero on her score sheet. "Fiddlesticks," she cursed to herself.

"Son-of-a-bitch! Playing Yahtzee. If that doesn't bring back the memories."

"Nu…er…Uncle Teddy, you haven't changed a bit," Joanna lied. *Yikes! Time has not been your friend, Dude.*

"Nice to see you, Joanna," he said as he pulled a handkerchief from his pocket and mopped the sweat from his face. "Wow, you look older than when I last saw you," he finished as he hobbled to the couch, plopped down beside Ruth and extended his hand toward Peanut. The dog approached with wagging tail, licked Teddy's hand, and plopped down on the floor near his feet almost as if the dog was imitating his owner.

"Teddy, you just saw me a week ago on Skype," Joanna said as she gave him a curious look.

"Mind if I join you, for old times' sake?" Before Joanna could reply he said, "Hey, I heard a good joke today. What did the pet bird say when he saw his owner reading the newspaper?" Then under his breath he said, "Pause for comic effect." He paused and then answered, "Why are you staring at the carpeting?" He laughed at himself and picked up the dice.

Oh, Teddy, you're still nutty after all these years. Joanna was pretty sure she'd heard that joke when she was a kid, and it wasn't really that funny to her then. During the summer that Joanna stayed with Ruth, Teddy had been "between jobs," whatever that meant, with a lot of free time on his hands. It seemed that he had been at Ruth's house a lot, sometimes helping out with chores but often simply visiting. Joanna remembered long, lazy afternoons spent with both Ruth and Teddy. That was when she had started thinking of him as Nutty Uncle Teddy.

Seeing him in person after all these years and being heartily greeted by him, Joanna couldn't help feeling a little rebellious against her mother. Beverly had not approved of Teddy's carefree lifestyle.

"For God's sake, Mother, he's a grown man. He should be out earning a living, not playing games all day," Joanna had once overheard her mother reprimanding her grandmother.

"Oh, Beverly, dear. He loves to play games with us," was Ruth's weak defense.

"Well, I forbid it. I will not have my ten-year old daughter exposed to all Teddy's flaky behaviors," Beverly hissed. "Do you understand me?"

It had been a long time, but Joanna still held a bit of resentment toward her mother for forbidding her to interact with Teddy. It wasn't necessarily that Beverly had forbidden it that upset Joanna; it was *how* Beverly had gone about it, purposely trying to humiliate Teddy. Now as an adult, Joanna could see that irresponsible Uncle Teddy wasn't the best example for a child. But, for Beverly to tell Teddy to his face that she didn't care for his influence on her daughter seemed really cruel. And, even worse, Joanna was sure her mother had meant for those words to inflict a wound.

After that, Teddy was rarely around. If he did happen to come over, it was to mow the lawn or fix something. Joanna sighed and shook her head as she remembered her mother's disdain toward Teddy. She wondered what had happened to Nutty Uncle Teddy to make him work-adverse while her mother was so addicted to it. Maybe it had something to do with an accident Teddy had while working as a bricklayer; but one thing was sure, Teddy was just wired differently than her mother.

Pushing the past from her mind, she said, "Want to play the next round, Teddy?"

"Sounds like just what the doctor ordered. But, hold that thought while I run into the kitchen and put some of the groceries I brought into the fridge."

"I'll do it," Joanna volunteered, wondering what it would look like to see Teddy attempt to run into the kitchen. "Do either of you want anything while I'm up?"

"I brought Grandma some Oreos. How about we break those open?" Teddy suggested.

Stepping over a now comatose Peanut, Joanna went into the kitchen. Next to the refrigerator, she found the groceries Teddy had left on the counter—mostly sweets, and also a bag of dried beans, a bunch of green grapes, a carton of orange juice, some yogurt, a jar of wheat bran, and, of course, the Oreos. She surveyed the goods for a snack and settled on the grapes, dismissing Teddy's desire for Oreos.

There was no doubt that Teddy was out of the ordinary. Joanna recalled one time when she had asked him why he wasn't married. Her ten-year-old mind had difficulty comprehending that marriage was not always an option for everyone. Besides in her child-like rationale, Teddy was fun and would probably make some woman very happy. To her question Teddy had given some silly response, but when she kept pressing him for a serious answer, she was startled and caught off guard when he suddenly grabbed her hand, bent down on one knee, and asked, "Ok, then. Joanna, will you marry me?" She realized later that he had meant it as a joke, but she was sufficiently shocked and said the first thing that occurred to her, "Eww, no! You're an old man." As soon as the words were out of her mouth, she regretted them, but the damage had been done. Or, so she thought. Teddy seemed unfazed by her cruel remark.

"All done with the groceries," said Joanna as she re-entered the living room with a bowl of grapes. "Thought these grapes looked too good to pass up." She paused as she set them down on the coffee table. A serious look came over her face. "Grandma," she confessed, "I'm sorry, but as I was putting away the groceries, one of the tomatoes fell to the floor. Splat!" She paused looking remorseful. Then with a twinkle in her eye, she added. "How do you fix a broken tomato?" Then under her breath she said, "Pause for comic effect." She paused and then answered herself, "with tomato paste!"

Chapter 10

On the morning after her doctor's appointment, Ruth limped into Joanna's bedroom and scooched up onto the bed without the aid of the walker.

"Careful, Grandma. Remember Dr. Killian said you could *start* to put weight on that foot."

"Is that what you're going to wear today, Dear?"

Joanna looked down at herself. She was dressed in jeans and a cropped t-shirt—one of her favorites. "Yes, that's my plan," Joanna replied. Then noticing the pained look on Ruth's face, she asked, "Grandma, are you okay on the edge of the bed? Here, let me get a box for under your foot. You still shouldn't have it down too much, because it will swell more." Joanna turned away from Ruth then squatted down to grab a box at the side of the bed.

"Ahem," Ruth cleared her throat.

Still squatting, Joanna turned her head toward Ruth and asked, "Are you okay, Grandma?"

Ruth said nothing. Joanna noticed that Ruth's head was slightly bowed, and her eyes were darting around in her head as though she was trying to indicate something with them while at the same time trying not to draw attention to that same something.

Joanna shifted her squatted weight from the ball of one foot to the other and bobbed her head toward Ruth as though the motion would help to control Ruth's ricocheting eyes and loosen Ruth's tongue, but all Joanna got was another, "Ahem," from Ruth with more crazy eye shifting.

"Grandma, what is it?" Joanna finally snapped as she shifted her crouching weight, trying to keep her feet from falling asleep as she waited for Ruth's reply.

"Well, dear, I don't like to mention it," Ruth hesitated, "but it looks like your underwear is coming apart." She flushed and her roving eyes settled briefly on Joanna's backside, and then darted quickly away as if she might be doomed to hell for gazing upon such an unseemly sight.

"What?" Joanna asked as she scrunched up her face, trying to hide her irritation. "My underwear isn't coming apart."

"Yes. It's like the waistband has separated," Ruth repeated, this time in a whisper. "It reminds me of a sanitary belt. Oh! Is that what it is? I've noticed you've been a little irritable today, dear. Maybe we should stop for a bit. You stretch out on the davenport, and I'll fix up the hot water bottle for your tummy. Never failed to bring me relief when I was menstruating."

"What?" Joanna sputtered again as she sprang to her feet. Then smiling with perception, Joanna said, "I'm not on the rag, and I'm not wearing a sanitary belt. That's a thong, Grandma."

"Oh," said Ruth, her voice rising as she feigned understanding.

"You know, a thong," Joanna repeated.

Ruth looked confused and uncomfortable.

Joanna lifted Ruth's leg up onto the box, and then walked to her suitcase. She returned and held out a red nylon thong for Ruth to examine.

"Oh," Ruth said again as she suddenly took an interest in the Kleenex she was subconsciously shredding into her lap.

"Grandma, everybody wears these. Here," said Joanna, "it won't bite you. You should try it on. You just might like it. I have to admit, it took a little getting used to, but now I love my thongs. No panty line. No creeping elastic," grinned Joanna. "See," she angled her rear end toward Ruth, a bit giddy that she had the upper hand in Ruth's discomfort. "And, it makes me feel sexy—you know, like a girl."

"But, you are a girl," Ruth offered. She frowned in Joanna's direction but still avoided looking at the white thong Joanna was wearing.

"No, I mean it makes me feel feminine," said Joanna. "Why did my thong make you think I have my period?" asked Joanna suddenly, now her turn to blush and feel uneasy.

"Oh, well, it's just that it looked like you were wearing a sanitary belt to hold your pad in place. It's been years since I was…" Ruth paused, pursed her lips, and then whispered, "Well, fertile. But, that's what it reminded me of."

"Hmm," Joanna replied. "I think I did hear my mom mention how thankful she was when self-adhesive pads came out so she didn't have to mess with that belt thing."

Ruth stared down at her hands, still shredding the already shredded Kleenex.

"I'm sorry, Grandma," Joanna apologized. "I didn't mean to make you uncomfortable."

"No, Dear. I was just thinking how thankful I was to the inventor of the sanitary belt. My mother used to shred old flour sacks, old dish towels, worn out dresses, whatever cloth material she could get her hands on. We girls used to pin those rags into our panties to soak up the flow—although it didn't always work. And Mother was always washing and drying those rags for us to reuse. With three girls plus Mother in the family, it was such a pleasure to have a disposable napkin and a garter belt to hold it in place."

"All I can say is, thank goodness for tampons!"

"Oh, dear, look at the time!" Ruth suddenly gasped. "Are you going to change?"

Joanna turned to check her rear view in the full-length mirror on the back of the bedroom door. She could just get a glimpse of the thong over the waistband of her pants when she bent or turned. She knew that it bothered her grandmother, but they were, after all, just going to the grocery store.

"Oh, come on, Grandma. No one at Wegman's cares about my thong."

"Well, yes dear, but first I thought we'd go out for lunch. At that restaurant over in Somerville—Scampi's."

"Oh, Grandma, we've driven by there. They don't have a dress code."

"Well, yes dear, but we might bump into some of my lady friends from the S.C.R.U."

"From the Screw?" Joanna eyed Ruth suspiciously.

"Yes. The Somerset County Retailers Union."

"What do you mean, 'bump into'?"

"Oh, I'm sure I told you. Today is our annual luncheon. We've met for more than 50 years…at noon… Don't worry, it's Dutch treat."

"That's fine," Joanna replied. "I'll drop you off and then come back for you. What time do you think you'll be done? 1:30? 2:00?"

Ruth put on a distraught face, looking rather like a sad little puppy dog.

Oh, boy. Here we go. Joanna had a hard time resisting her grandmother's forlorn look, and she knew that Ruth knew it.

"Grandma, I don't know any of your lady friends. I'll just be in the way."

"Please come with me, Joanna," Ruth sulked.

"Grandma, lunch with your lady friends isn't on today's agenda for me," Joanna countered, trying to keep annoyance out of her voice. "Besides, your friends might not like me if they knew I wore a thong."

"You're sounding just like your mother. If I didn't know better, I'd think Beverly was standing right here in this room with us. My Beverly never was one for doing something at the spur of the moment. Always afraid of what people might think of her."

Joanna rolled her eyes – more to herself than at her Grandmother - took a deep breath and said, "OK, I'll go, but only because I love you." She could feel butterflies stirring in her stomach. It made her somewhat nervous to meet new people. *But really, what do I have to lose*, she asked herself. Joanna knew Ruth would delight in showing off her only granddaughter to all of her friends. On the one hand, Joanna had to admit to herself that she did kind of like the attention Ruth and her friends were sure to shower upon her, but at the same time, she wasn't at all sure what she would say to women four times her age. But, mostly she could not abide the comparison to her mother…and she knew Ruth knew it too.

"Don't you think you'd like to put on something a little more…"

"Conservative?" asked Joanna.

"Well, it's a bit chilly today, and you may have to help Berta and Lurena in and out of the car."

"Who?"

"Berta and Lurena."

"Grandma, I don't know those people."

"Yes, you do. Well, Berta anyway. She goes to my church, and you went to church with me every Sunday during that summer you stayed with me."

"I was ten."

"And, Lurena used to babysit your mom when she was a baby. She's practically family." Ruth put her arm around Joanna's shoulder and gave her a quick squeeze. "It will be fun, Sweetie. You'll see." Joanna rummaged through her suitcase and found a longer t-shirt. Plain. White. Boring. She thought about changing out of her jeans, but decided that agreeing to go to the luncheon was enough of a sacrifice. She'd be physically comfortable at lunch if nothing else.

Chapter 11

As Joanna locked the house, Ruth opened the driver's side door to the car and said, "You'd better let me drive."
Joanna protested, but Ruth was pulling on Joanna's arm and saying, "Now Dearie, I've been driving longer than you are old. I know these streets like the back of my hand. Come on. Get in."

Joanna hated it when people referred to how much older and wiser they were, but she reluctantly climbed in on the passenger's side. "Everyone buckled up?" Ruth asked as she revved the engine and pulled abruptly into the street.

Hope we make it home alive! Joanna panicked inwardly.

Two blocks later, they pulled into the driveway of a home that looked less cared for than Ruth's house. No sooner had the car settled into park than a tiny woman with a severely hunched back emerged from the hovel in front of them. She locked the door from which she had just exited and shuffled along the walk to the car. "Hi, Berta," Ruth called out as she opened her window and waved. Startled by Berta's agility, but fearful that the petite, convex-shaped woman might trip and fall, Joanna sprang from the car and offered Berta an arm.

"Oh, thank you, dear." She smiled up at Joanna from her awkwardly cocked stance. "You must be Ruth's granddaughter. You look just like her."

Joanna opened the back driver's side door as she responded, "Yes, I'm Joanna. Nice to meet you." She extended her hand toward Berta only to be ignored, as Berta reached through the open driver's window and grabbed Ruth's hand.

"Good to see you Ruthie!" croaked Berta matter-of-factly.

"You too, Bertie," Ruth answered as she pulled Berta's hand to her lips for quick kiss.

With her hand still out-stretched, Joanna frowned then smirked at Berta's refusal of her greeting. Agitation crept into Joanna's thoughts. *It's lovely to meet you too, Joanna. So good of you to give up your day to babysit the old ladies!* While Ruth and Berta completed their greeting, Joanna stood at the open back door like a chauffeur.

Finally, Berta shuffled past Joanna, then slowly lifted one leg into the car, painstakingly scooted her backside onto the seat, and drew her second leg in after her. "I am in the car. You may close the door, Hanna, " Berta shouted.

"This is going to be such fun," Joanna mumbled under her breath as she rounded the back of the car and hopped into the front seat next to Ruth.

"Seatbelts, everyone?" asked Ruth. "Next stop Lurena's," she added merrily.

"Oh, I haven't seen Lurena in…I bet it's going on two years," commented Berta. "How is she doing, you know, after her trauma?"

"Oh, poor Lurena. Henry's death was such a shock to her. But, you know Lurena. She's a fighter. Doesn't let anything get her down. That man was nothing but trouble for her. God knows why, but she did love him. And, he did provide nicely for her."

"Oh, yes, it is such a treat that she can afford to live over at Shady Oaks."

After a 15-minute drive, Ruth maneuvered the car into the circle drive at Shady Oaks. It was a repeat performance of the Berta pick-up, except that this time the stooped over woman was taller but walked even more slowly and with a cane, which she seemed to knock into everything—the bushes, a crack in the sidewalk, the empty flower planters. Joanna once again resumed the role of aide and escorted Lurena to the car, dropping Lurena's arm only long enough to open the back passenger side door for her.

"New car, Ruthie?" Lurena asked as she grabbed the front passenger side door handle, swung open the door, and folded herself into the front seat next to Ruth. Joanna stood in the driveway holding the rear door open, astonished by what she had just witnessed.

"Oh, no. This is Teddy's car. Mine is acting up again, don't you know." She and Lurena hugged across the gearshift. "Joanna, time's a wasting." Ruth called out to Joanna over her shoulder as she revved the engine. Joanna leapt into the backseat next to Berta, who was still fumbling with her seatbelt.

"Can I help?" Joanna asked, to which she received no response. "Can I help you with your seatbelt?" she tried again.

"Berta's a bit hard of hearing," Lurena practically hollered from the front seat. "DO YOU WANT HELP WITH YOUR SEAT BELT, BERTIE?" Lurena broadcasted with full force into the backseat.

"Thank you, dear," Berta said demurely as she handed the seatbelt to Joanna. Looking down at where it should buckle, Joanna saw nothing.

Realizing that Berta must be sitting on top of the belt buckle, Joanna said, "Ma'am, I think the buckle is underneath you," to which Berta made no reply.

With Ruth revving the engine, Joanna realized the urgency in getting Berta belted in. She tapped Berta's shoulder, smiled at her, and tried again. "Ma'am, I think the buckle is stuck down in the seat."

Berta looked over at Joanna and returned the smile. "I'm famished too. I can't wait to eat."

"Right," Joanna said then realizing she had no other alternative, she hollered, "I THINK THE BUCKLE IS UNDERNEATH YOU." Berta responded by leaning to one side and slightly raising her backside for Joanna, who snatched the buckle and snapped it into the receptacle.

After about 20 minutes in the car—during which Joanna merely listened to the conversation, having given up speaking in fear of losing her voice—Ruth pulled up at the front of Scampi's Restaurant in Somerville and double-parked. "I'll let you girls off here and then go around the block to find a spot." Berta and Lurena dutifully, albeit slowly, began to unbuckle. Joanna immediately hopped out of the car, intending to open Lurena's car door for her. But the squealing of tires and a blaring horn alerted Joanna to the door on Berta's side protruding out into traffic. Circling the back of the car, Joanna was just in time to direct traffic around Berta's open door and watch as Berta shuffled around the car and up onto the curb. Joanna was amazed. *For such a tiny little woman, she sure has a lot of energy.*

Not really wanting to babysit the 'girls' and not quite trusting her grandmother with the task of parallel parking, Joanna insisted that she take the car and park it. Opening Ruth's door and unbuckling her seatbelt, Joanna took Ruth by the elbow and gently guided her out of the car.

"Grandma, look, Berta and Lurena are waiting for you," she said as she ushered Ruth toward the curb where Berta and Lurena stood waving. Ruth tottered over to her friends, and Joanna was relieved when she saw an older gentleman hold the door. "Good day, lovely ladies," he said as he tipped his hat. The girls giggled and blushed. *Cute,* Joanna thought as she watched, but the guy in the car behind her didn't seem to think the double-parked car in front of him was so cute. He laid on his horn, startling Joanna into action.

Joanna jumped back in the car, and circled the block only once, managing to secure a spot nearly at Scampi's front door. She slugged the meter and dashed inside, asking the hostess for the location of the ladies' luncheon. Receiving an odd look, Joanna told the hostess somewhat impatiently, "I'm not here because I want to be. "I'm here with my grandma."

Without saying a word, the hostess directed Joanna toward the back of the restaurant to a long table with about ten gray-haired women seated around it. Seeing no available seat, Joanna smiled to herself, more than willing to make some excuse about checking out the consignment shop next to the restaurant. But, there was no need for an excuse. As soon as Ruth saw her, she insisted on having everyone's attention, stood and held Joanna's hand, announcing, "Everyone, this is my granddaughter, Joanna, Beverly's girl. She's here visiting me."

A waiter appeared with a chair, and Joanna scooted into it between Ruth and Lurena.

As Joanna hid behind her menu, she noticed Ruth squirming in her seat. Joanna leaned close to her grandmother and asked, "Are you okay?"

Ruth answered, "Yes, dear. I'm fine," as she continued to shift from side to side.

Puzzled by Ruth's odd behavior, Joanna continued to probe, "Is your foot hurting, Grandma?"

"No. My foot is fine."

Unconvinced, Joanna leaned over to peer under the table at Ruth's foot but was distracted by someone poking her from behind. Turning her head, Joanna discovered Lurena facing her with open mouth as if to say something. Expecting Lurena to whisper a greeting or heap praise on her for visiting with Ruth, Joanna turned her ear toward Lurena and leaned in closer.

"CAN YOU TAKE ME TO THE BATHROOM?" Lurena shouted into Joanna's ear.

Confused and unsure of what to say, Joanna softly said, "What?" which prompted an even louder appeal.

"CAN YOU TAKE ME TO THE BATHROOM?"

The request, in and of itself, embarrassed Joanna, but the volume of its delivery was downright mortifying. Joanna sprang from her chair to help Lurena up if for no other reason than to avert further broadcasts.

"Are you headed to the ladies' room?" asked Ruth. "I'll go with you." With Lurena clinging on to one of Joanna's arms and

Ruth on the other, the three of them shuffled into the restroom. Joanna wondered what Lurena's request to "take me to the bathroom" actually meant. *Does she expect me to go into the stall with her? Should I ask her or just leave her at the door? What if she needs to be wiped?* Joanna shuddered as she opened the stall door for Lurena.

"THIS IS FINE, DEAR. YOU CAN WAIT OUT HERE. DON'T NEED ANYBODY IN THERE WITH ME …YET."

Relieved, Joanna stood leaning against the sink for what seemed an extremely long time.

Meanwhile Ruth emerged and made her way over to the sink to wash her hands. As she leaned forward, slightly aiming her backside toward Joanna, she said, "Sooo… what do you think?

Joanna whispered to Ruth, "Should I crack the door open and ask if she's ok or do I just wait?"

"Lurena will be fine," said Ruth. "I mean what do you think about my new look?"

Joanna, still distracted about what was going on behind the stall door, whispered, "What if she's fallen?" Alarmed at the thought of Lurena needing help, Joanna leaned down to check underneath the stall. The sound of the toilet flushing eased Joanna's mind, and soon enough, Joanna saw the door budge a bit as Lurena struggled with it from the inside. Luckily, it swung outward, so that Joanna could slowly pull it open without knocking Lurena to the floor.

As they left the restroom, Lurena commented more to herself than to Joanna, "Oh, that was lovely. To be able to have a BM with no one rushing me or checking on me every five seconds is heavenly." And then to Joanna she proclaimed, "THANK YOU, DEAR. IF YOU EVER HAVE A HANKERING FOR A JOB, SHADY OAKS COULD USE SOMEONE JUST LIKE YOU. YOU COULD TEACH SOME OF THE FOLKS WE HAVE ON STAFF A THING OR TWO ABOUT PRIVACY."

Privacy? Joanna wondered to herself. *You just announced to the whole restaurant that you were heading to the crapper and then told me about your bowel movement. Privacy? Whatever.* She sighed to herself and rolled her eyes behind Lurena.

Ruth nudged Joanna. Thinking she was caught, Joanna immediately ceased her eye roll, not wanting to offend her grandmother. Ruth nudged Joanna again. "I just had to make an adjustment in there," she said as she lifted her blouse to waist level on one side, revealing a thin strip of red satin against her skin.

Pushing Ruth's blouse back down, Joanna whispered, "Grandma, we're in public!" Then she saw the twinkle in Ruth's eye.

As Ruth smoothed her blouse, she winked. "It makes me feel young again, don't you know. 'Like a girl.'" Surprised, but equally amused, Joanna giggled.

Chapter 12

To Joanna, the ladies luncheon at Scampi's was worse than she could have imagined, but she had to admit it had gotten her out of the house and away from the unending task of trying to de-clutter her grandmother's house. Now back at home, she sighed and resigned herself to the task of tidying up. However, before she could decide what to tackle, she was interrupted by a text: "hows nj"

Deborah's text was a welcome relief, but Joanna struggled with how to answer. *Gmas fine? Things r weird? This is harder than I thought?* Not sure what to say, she dialed Deborah.

"What's up, Miss Joanna?" Deborah answered, sounding upbeat and almost giddy.

Oblivious to Deborah's good mood, Joanna moaned, "Please tell me I've been dreaming and that I'm really back on campus."

"Oh no, you don't want to be here."

"Why not? It seems to be pretty good for your state of mind. I feel like I've died and gone to housekeeping hell."

"Going to New Jersey was your idea, wasn't it?"

"Yeah, I know. I guess I just didn't really know what I was signing up for."

"Really? It's just you and your grandma. How hard can it be? She's such a sweet, little old lady."

"Well, of course, she is. But, that's not the point. I thought I'd be able to chill out with her and clear my head, you know. But, she has so much stuff. Like so much stuff, I'm afraid she's going to trip and fall again. I've been trying to organize her things by sorting them into piles, like stuff to keep, stuff for donation, stuff to throw away, stuff to recycle...but the trouble is that if Grandma is anywhere nearby, she tries to save everything, even though most of it isn't even worthy to be called trash.

"Like, I'll put old magazines in the recycle pile, and she'll go, 'Oh, our library takes old magazines. Let's drive those over there later this afternoon, shall we?' Or, I'll put some ratty old blanket in the garbage pile, and she'll say, 'I think I'll save that for my friend, Mildred. She could probably use it.' Or, I'll pick up something that is obviously broken, and before I can make a move, she'll say, 'That old clock doesn't really keep time any more, but my Aunt Beulah gave that to me when I graduated from high school. I could never get rid of that.'

"Sometimes I just want to scream 'Everything does not have significance!' But, to my grandma, it does. It's just so frustrating! Every time I think I'm done sorting through things in one area, I find more stuff piled on a chair or in a closet, or something that has been stashed behind a dresser that looks like her clothes could get caught on it, or another box crammed under a bed that looks like it could trip her. "

"Wow, you kind of make her sound like a hoarder."

"Well, no. Not like the people you see on TV or hear about on the news. Grandma just has all of this stuff she's accumulated over the years, that seems meaningless… except to her." Joanna let out a long breath. "I think I'm kind of regretting my offer to help."

"Wow, Jo, you sound kind of stressed."

"Yeah, I am stressed. When am I ever going to get some time for myself?" Joanna whined more to herself than to Deborah.

"Hey, why don't you get your uncle to help? I thought he lived close by."

"Oh yeah, right. Nutty Uncle Teddy. He's over here all the time pretending to help, but all he really does is watch TV and feed Grandma sugar. If I ask him to help me with something, he fakes some sort of injury or suddenly has to go home, probably to play on-line poker—which is all it seems like he ever does with any enthusiasm. I'm just not making any progress. I would have been better off staying in Illinois."

"But, I thought the reason you decided to go out there was for your grandma, not for you. Why don't you take a break? I have an idea…"

"Yeah, you're right, I should, but this is driving me crazy. I'm just feeling so much pressure to get this done for Grandma."

As Joanna drew in another breath intending to continue her tirade, her phone beeped. It was her dad—another needy person in her life.

"I got another call. Sorry I gotta' take this, Deb."

"Yeah, ok. No problem. Just promise me one thing: call me back."

"Ok, sure. I'll talk to you later," Joanna answered absentmindedly as she switched the call to her dad.

"Hey, Dad."

"Have you reconsidered coming to Nana's with me?"

"Well, Dad, here's the thing. I can't leave Grandma right now, she still needs me."

"But, Teddy's there. Surely he can handle things with Grandma for a few days."

"Well, yeah, normally he could," Joanna rolled her eyes as she lied about Teddy's ability to take responsibility for anything. *What I am doing? Lying to my dad?* Joanna wondered, but then added more to her fib. "But, Uncle Teddy just got a part time job, so he's not around as much right now."

"Really?" Peter asked, sounding confused. "Teddy got a job?"

"Yeah, it's some seasonal thing, and his schedule is kind of unpredictable, so he can't always be available when Grandma needs him."

In her own mind, Joanna tried to rationalize that what she was telling her dad was true. The parts about Teddy being unpredictable and Grandma not being able to count on him were both true. And, to a certain extent, the part about Teddy having a job was true, if you could call house sitting for the weekend for Mrs. Jones across the street a seasonal job. So, Joanna concluded to herself, in an admittedly warped kind of way, that she wasn't really lying to her dad after all.

"I'm sorry, Dad," Joanna feigned her disappointment. "I know how much you were looking forward to our visit with Nana." She paused, trying to figure out a way to get off of the phone; the discomfort of saying no to her dad by lying to him was sharpening by the moment.

Filling the awkward silence, Peter asked with just a tinge of hurt laced around his words, "And, you were looking forward to it too, weren't you, Joanna?"

"Of course, I was, Dad. But, I can't leave Grandma right now. You understand, don't you?"

"Oh, well, of course I understand, Kiddo. I'm just being selfish. There will be other times for the three of us to be together. Grandma Ruth is getting up there in age. Of course, so is Nana, but Grandma Ruth needs you right now, so you have to do what you have to do. Nana and I will get along without you. Happy Thanksgiving, Sweetie."

Talk about heaping on the guilt. If those comments had come from her mother, Joanna would have suspected them as a plot to change her mind. But, she knew that her Dad was genuinely disappointed, which made her lie all the more painful.

"Thanks for understanding, Dad. Happy Thanksgiving to you. And to Nana, too."

She ended the call with an overwhelming sense of guilt sitting in the pit of her stomach. *Some daughter I am,* she chastised herself. She tried to free her mind of any regrets she had about the just-ended phone call by focusing on the work in front of her. Joanna shuffled around looking for the best plan of attack. Then, throwing up her arms, she said out loud, "I give up." It seemed like she was getting nowhere. *Guess I'm not much in the granddaughter department either.*

Absorbed in her thoughts, she didn't hear her grandmother's footsteps coming down the hall.

"Joanna dear, you've been working so hard. It's time to take a break and have some supper. I fixed us up some leftovers."

Crap. I hope Grandma didn't hear what I was just saying on the phone.

Motioning to the pile of her possessions sitting on and around the trash can, Ruth asked, "What are these doing here?" Then, picking up several yellowed pieces of paper from the heap, she smiled, "Teddy made these finger-paintings for me when he was in kindergarten. Aren't they wonderful? I keep meaning to hang them up," she said more to herself than to Joanna. With the papers still in hand, she turned toward the closet. "I think there are some frames in here somewhere."

Joanna drew in a deep breath and sighed. *Alrighty, then. Still focused on the junk. She must not have heard me.*

And then, before Ruth could comment on anything else, Joanna ushered her grandmother out of the bedroom.

Chapter 13

After dinner, Joanna said, "I'm thinking of some ice cream, Grandma. How about you?"

"That's just what I want, too," Ruth replied.

"I'll get it Grandma," Joanna insisted. "You go have a seat in the living room."

"Sounds good to me, sweetie," Ruth answered with a wink and a yawn. "I'd help you, but I'm feeling a bit sleepy tonight."

"That's ok," countered Joanna, "I've got it." She turned on the TV and made sure Ruth was comfortable.

With the lights down low in the living room and nothing to illuminate her way but the glow of the television, Joanna carefully shuffled along toward the kitchen, her feet making a zzit-zzit sound along the plastic runner. It made her smile as she recalled the joy this action brought to her as a young girl and also smirk at the thought of how upset it made her mom, "For heaven's sake Joanna, pick up your feet when you walk," was Beverly's usual commentary.

"You'll find the ice cream dishes in the cabinet just to the right of the sink," Ruth said. "But, oh dear, I'm not sure if there's any ice cream." Ruth's comments trailed off as Joanna stood in front of the Frigidaire – the same one she remembered from years ago. Tugging at the freezer, then giving it a good yank, Joanna was not prepared for the avalanche of food that careened out and onto the floor. She jumped back just in time to spare her toes from being crushed by a chubby roll of Jimmy Dean's Pure Pork Sausage.

"Everything ok, sweet pea?" Ruth called from the other room.

"I'm good," yelled Joanna as a box of frozen spinach crashed to the floor and sent the ice encasing it in all directions across the kitchen.

"Well, hurry back. *Breakfast at Tiffany's* is on. They sure don't make movies like that any more."

Cautiously, Joanna peered inside the freezer while holding her hand in front of its remaining contents. It seemed geometrically impossible that all of the food now on the floor had at one time been contained within the freezer, which had spewed out some of its innards, but still appeared to be full. *How can that be?* Joanna wondered. Rather than contemplate it further and risk missing any more of the movie, Joanna burrowed around in the frozen compartment of the Fridgaire until she found three tubs of ice cream: vanilla - *Why bother*; butter pecan – *Better, but not very exciting*; and Neapolitan - *Hmm…fairly boring, but at least there's some chocolate in there.* Pulling the Neapolitan from the freezer and carefully placing the food from the floor back inside, Joanna felt her stomach rumble as it anticipated the ice cream soon to be sent down to it. And then, she shuddered as one of her mother's favorite expressions visited her, "Eat when you are upset, and you'll be upset when you get on the scale in the morning."

Ruth's feeble holler from the next room, "The show is coming on again," prompted Joanna to jolt her food service skills into high gear. She opened the cabinet to the right of the sink and grabbed two ice cream parlor style dishes, the ones she remembered from her childhood. She smiled at the memory and then quickly reached for the Neapolitan. Opening the lid, Joanna furrowed her brow and said aloud, "How long has she had this?" and tossed the crystallized container into the sink.

"Let's try this again," she said as she carefully extracted the butter pecan from the freezer. "Hmm…I think this one's even older," she concluded as she tossed this carton as well.

"Third time's a charm…or maybe not." Joanna peered down at the gooey mass that had once been vanilla ice cream as she snatched two bananas from the lazy Susan on the kitchen table and went back to join Ruth and Audrey and George.

"Thought I'd grab something a bit healthier than ice cream," Joanna commented. But as she handed Ruth the piece of fruit, she noticed that her grandmother had fallen asleep and was softly snoring to the rhythm of Holly Golightly strumming *Moon River* on the guitar.

As Joanna sat in the dark, munching her banana and trying to pay attention to the film, her phone rang. It was Deborah. Joanna picked up.

"Hey, Deb. Oh sorry, I forgot to call you back. I got distracted by stuff here…"

"Hey, Jo, it's okay." Deborah sounded excited. "I just need to tell you my good news. Wanna meet me in New York City tomorrow?"

"Good one," Joanna responded. "That would be some drive to get from Illinois to New York overnight."

"Yeah, well, that's the thing. My dad surprised us with a quick trip to the Big Apple for Thanksgiving. Apparently he's been planning it for some time. He booked a fancy Thanksgiving reservation for us, but tomorrow everyone is going to do their own thing. So, naturally, I thought of you."

"Wow, Deb, that would be great," Joanna started, "but I really can't get away right now."

"Why can't you meet me in New York? You said it yourself that you needed a break from your grandma, or from cleaning your grandma's house."

"Yeah, I know, but leaving Grandma's the problem."

"Oh, so I'm a problem now, am I?" asked Ruth, feigning wounded pride.

Joanna turned to see a glint in Ruth's eyes. "Um, ok, Deb," she said. "I'll see what I can do. Text me the directions."

Turning to Ruth, Joanna said, "Oh come on, Grandma. That's not fair. You're not a problem."

"Well, you just said that I was."

"No, I meant that I wouldn't be able to meet my friend Deborah in New York City tomorrow."

"I used to work in the city—don't you know," Ruth replied with a far-off look in her eye. "Took the train in every day. Rode the subway all by myself. Walked to work down 5th Avenue—in high heels, no less."

"Really," Joanna murmured, somewhat distracted by her thoughts as she pondered who she could get to stay with her grandmother. "Do you think Teddy is doing anything tomorrow?" she said more to herself than to Ruth. Then, turning to Ruth and smiling, she continued, "I bet Teddy would be willing to spend the day with you tomorrow."

"Yes, I suppose so…But, you know, we could all go into the city together," Ruth suggested slyly.

"Sure," Joanna answered, scrolling through her contact list for Teddy's number. "Wait, what? What do you mean – we?"

"You and me and Teddy. We could all go into town and meet Deborah. You talk so much about her, it would be such a treat to finally meet her in person. She sounds like such a delightful girl."

"Grandma, it's been forever since Deborah and I have had a chance to really talk. We kind of wanted to, you know, catch up on things privately."

"Well, of course, dear. You girls could spend the day together, while Teddy and I take in the city, and then we'll all meet up for a big meal. I know this marvelous Chinese restaurant in Central Park South. They make a soup dumpling that is really quite tasty."

Joanna sighed as she dialed Teddy. "Hello?" was his cautious answer.

"Hey, Teddy. Doing anything tomorrow?"

"Not a thing sweet pea." He perked up at the sound of Joanna's voice. "What's up?"

"Well, how would you like to spend the day with Grandma tomorrow?"

"Well, sure, sweetheart. You know I can't resist spending time with my two favorite girls."

"Well, that's the thing," Joanna stammered. "I'm heading into New York City to visit a friend, and I need someone to stay with Grandma while I'm gone."

"Oh," Teddy hesitated. "I see." He paused, leaving a brief awkward silence on the phone. Then, somewhat deflated, he continued. "I guess I could peek in on her now and then tomorrow, but you know, I do have my own things to do."

Yeah, like playing Internet poker all day. She inhaled softly, rolled her eyes, and slowly let out her breath. "Teddy, come on, you know I'd take you and Grandma with me if I could, but…"

That was just the small foothold Teddy needed. Joanna realized her mistake only after it was out of her mouth, and it was too late to take it back.

"Oh, but you can take us with you," Teddy quickly interjected. "We won't be any trouble. You and your friend can visit, and Ma and me will do our own thing."

Joanna sighed again, not knowing what to say. She knew that leaving Ruth at home with Teddy's promise to occasionally check in on her was a disaster waiting to happen. If Teddy actually did remember to look in on Ruth as promised, Joanna pictured the likely scenario of her waiting on him hand and foot, instead of the other way around.

"I don't know," Joanna hesitated. "She's not too steady on her feet yet."

"Are you kidding me?" Teddy interrupted. "Ma's just fine."

She sighed again as Teddy continued, "Well, Joanna? What do you think? Sounds like a fun time to me! What time do we leave?"

Joanna closed her eyes, drew in a third breath, and flatly replied, "Can you be here at 8?"

"You betcha," came Teddy's reply as she hung up.

Ruth's face was beaming with a satisfied, all-knowing look. "That's the one thing you have to remember about Teddy. When it comes to a day out on the town, Teddy's going to go, come heck or high water."

"Great," Joanna commented, admitting her defeat.

"Oh, now sweetie, it could be worse. Just think of the potential mess you would have had to clean up here tomorrow if Teddy was in charge all day." Ruth winked at Joanna as she exited the room.

Chapter 14

As if in keen awareness of Joanna's unsettled feelings about the day's activities, the morning sun was clouded over, forecasting a cold, blustery, and potentially precipitative November day. "Maybe this is a sign," Joanna said under her breath as she glanced out the window at the ominous day.

Even though Ruth had professed her expertise at riding the train and subway, Joanna made the executive decision that they would drive into New York. The GPS on her phone was fairly reliable, and she felt more confident in the abilities of a machine than the 50-year old recollections of her 79-year old grandmother. Teddy arrived at the door on schedule to avoid work – just after the car was packed. And then, before they headed out the door, Ruth reminded everyone, "Better go to the bathroom before we hit the road."

"I don't need to go," Teddy insisted.

"Well, the car doesn't go until you do," came Ruth's matter of fact reply.

What have I gotten myself into? Joanna watched mother and son banter back and forth, which finally resulted in Teddy stomping off to the bathroom.

With the three of them finally loaded and buckled in, Joanna steered the car toward New York City. *I hope this is worth it*, Joanna thought uneasily as she contemplated the trade off between the freedom of spending the day with Deborah and the responsibility of keeping tabs on Ruth and Teddy.

Despite her reservations, there was little traffic to speak of, considering they were on the New Jersey Turnpike. The congestion of vehicles at the entrance to the Lincoln Tunnel was bearable. Upon emerging from the tunnel, they scored a prime parking spot at the Port Authority on the top floor, right next to the elevator. Just as the sun peaked out from behind the clouds, Joanna had the feeling that it might be a pleasurable day, in spite of its odd and foreboding beginning.

Joanna helped her grandmother out of the car while Teddy huffed and puffed as he slowly extracted himself from the backseat. "Come on, Teddy!" Joanna prodded. "It's not that hard to get out of the car." Precariously perched on the edge of the seat, Teddy groaned. Noting the strain of his shirt buttons over his bulging belly, she suspected that his lethargy was a contrived tactic to avoid any gratuitous exertion of energy. Joanna shook her head. After a quick check to make sure that the car was locked, she herded her charges into the elevator and pushed the close door button.

Safely tucked inside, it was hard for Joanna to contain her excitement. She smiled at Ruth in delighted expectancy about the day ahead. On their descent, the elevator car continued to fill with other Port Authority parkers, until there was scant elbow-room for anyone. Teddy, however, was slumped in the corner and oblivious to the need for him to stand up straight in order to create more space for the newcomers. Joanna held on tightly to Ruth's arm in an effort to prevent accidental separation from her grandmother, as Ruth smiled sweetly and nodded a greeting at each new rider, even though she was generally ignored.

At one point during their ride down, Ruth announced to everyone in their car, "We're going to paint the town red, today." Yet no one seemed to acknowledge her remark, with the possible exception of a sharply dressed man in a business suit. Positioned at a perpendicular angle to Ruth, he held his morning coffee in one hand. In the other, he clutched *The Wall Street Journal* that he seemed to be reading with great interest. Upon hearing Ruth's comment, he raised one eyebrow, gave her a pained expression – like he'd just gotten a whiff of a rather offensive odor – and then he ceremoniously flipped his paper over and raised it higher, obscuring his face from hers. Nevertheless, Ruth appeared unaware of his spiteful act.

Shortly, the elevator doors slid open, spilling everyone out into the crowded main level of the Port Authority. Joanna saw the reader of the *Journal* stumble as he exited the car, and she noted the satisfied grin on Teddy's face as he gazed innocently up at the ceiling while repositioning his outstretched foot back on the floor underneath himself. She smiled to herself. It might have been a childish act, but, God love him, Teddy really did care about his mother.

The bustling activity in the Port Authority was exciting and, at the same time, intimidating to Joanna. She couldn't fathom how they would find Deborah in the beehive of commotion in front of them, but they managed to maneuver themselves outside and get to the corner of 8th Avenue and 42nd Street, their designated point of rendezvous with Deborah, and against all odds, there she was. Joanna was relieved to see her friend and enveloped Deborah in an emotional embrace.

"Yeah, Jo! You made it!"

Releasing her hold on Deborah, Joanna grinned. "Oh, it's so good to see you, Deb!"

"Well, hello, dear," Ruth said as she wormed her way in between the two friends and grabbed Deborah around the waist in a grandmotherly cuddle. "I feel like I already know you. Joanna has told me so much about you."

Startled but flattered, Deborah returned Ruth's hug. "It's nice to finally meet you in person, too, Mrs. Lathrop."

"Hey, you didn't say how attractive your friend was, Joanna," came Teddy's somewhat husky voice from behind her as he worked his way toward Deborah for his own hug.

"Oh. This is Teddy. My mom's brother," Joanna announced as she stepped into Teddy's path. "He's my uncle," she proclaimed through clenched teeth staring right at Teddy. "He's old enough to be your father," she enunciated more loudly. Although her comments were addressed to Deborah, she glared directly at Teddy as she spoke, causing him to back off.

Eager to strike out on her own with Deborah, Joanna quickly reviewed the plan for the day with Ruth and Teddy. "Madame Toussaud's is just around the corner, and then you can have lunch at the Olive Garden. Take a cab up to West 56th Street. Remember we have a 5:30 reservation at Joe's Shanghai. Here are the addresses and phone numbers and a Google map of the area. I've made one for each of you. Stay together and don't be late. Ok?"

"Geez, Joanna. You act like you don't trust me," said Teddy, sounding wounded.

Before Joanna could respond to Teddy's accusation, Ruth reassured her, "Don't worry sweetie. I've spent more than my fair share of time in this city. We'll be fine."

Joanna smiled back at Ruth. Then grabbing Teddy's face between her hands, thus stealing his gaze away from the buxom brunette he was ogling, she fixed her eyes on his and warned,

"Teddy, I need you to stick with Grandma today. Don't let her out of your sight. Got it?"

"No worries, Jo. Piece of cake. You and Debbers go and have a great time!" He returned her stare with a carefree smile. "Come on, Ma," he said as he extended his arm. Ruth beamed up at him and gave him a brief hug; then they proceeded to hobble off together down 42nd Street.

"Jo, are you sure you can trust them alone together?"

Joanna inhaled slowly, hesitated, and then reassured Deborah and herself that they would be fine.

"Cuz we can tag along with them if you want to," Deborah offered.

"No, trust me, it wouldn't be the same if we spent the day with them. It might be okay with just Grandma, but with Teddy…" she inhaled again and let her breath out slowly, "What can I say?"

Chapter 15

Their day together was a gift, just what Joanna needed as a pick-me-up from her responsibilities with her grandmother. They talked non-stop as they traversed the streets of the city. On the observation deck of the Empire State Building, Deborah pointed out where the Twin Towers had once stood, and Joanna caught site of the Statue of Liberty, Ellis Island, and the vast expanse of Central Park. They did some window-shopping along Fifth Avenue and even popped into Saks. Gasping and giggling at the extravagant prices they saw there, Joanna was reminded of the scene in *Breakfast at Tiffany's* where Holly Golightly and Paul Varjak tackle the nearly impossible task of trying to find something at Tiffany and Company that they can purchase for $10 or under.

"Let's go to Tiffany's," suggested Joanna.

"Of course," agreed Deborah. "It's right on our way to Central Park."

It was a beautiful store with tall ceilings, sparkling jewelry cases, and a cordial, but stoic doorman. *Or is he a security guard,*

Joanna wondered. The rather austere atmosphere inside the store made Joanna feel somewhat like a criminal, and she took care not to lean on the glass-topped counters. However, it *was* a magical place, and Joanna could appreciate Holly Golightly's fascination with it and all it stood for in her mind. As they exited the store, Joanna quoted Holly to Deborah, "If I could find a real life place that made me feel like Tiffany's, then I'd buy some furniture and give the cat a name."

Deborah gave her a queer look. "You don't even have a cat."

Joanna smiled at the thought of telling Ruth about her pleasant encounter with Tiffany's. "No, that's a quote from *Breakfast at Tiffany's*, Deb. You really need to see that movie. They don't make them like that anymore." Joanna smiled as she quoted her grandmother.

As they made their way toward Central Park, they walked arm in arm, which Joanna noticed was gleaning a few sideways glances from passers-by. When she mentioned the stares they were garnering, Deborah replied matter-of-factly. "Oh, they probably just think we're lesbians." Joanna was perplexed at encountering such rube-like attitudes in what could easily be argued the most cosmopolitan place on earth, but she refused to let it spoil her mood.

They entered the Park, and after walking for hours, they had covered but a small section of it. Exhausted, they found a seat on a bench along the Central Park Mall. As an occasional skate boarder careened precariously along the sidewalk in front of them, Joanna glanced at her watch, not ready to return to reality. It was 3:47. "Deb, how long will it take for us to get to dinner?"

"Hmm, I think about 20 minutes," was Deborah's estimate.

Joanna was thrilled that they had more time, but she experienced a feeling of guilt when she realized that she hadn't thought of Ruth or Teddy all day. *Oh well, it's my day. I'm sure they're having fun, too,* she told herself. She smiled, and then frowned, as she pondered the notion that she was really not looking forward to meeting up with her grandmother and uncle. However, as a few snowflakes began to flutter to the ground at her feet, and with the distant echo of horse and buggy rides surrounding her, Joanna was able to banish the thought from her mind. She sat in silence with her friend, continuing to bask in the delight of their day together in New York City.

When a young couple walked by arguing with one another about who was the better driver, Joanna shot them an unappreciative glare, annoyed at how the presumptuousness of their verbal exchange was interfering with the magic of her day. Fortunately, they were intent on making their way through the Mall, and soon their presence was a faint memory. But, that brief incident planted a burr of irritation in Joanna's thoughts. *Why do some people think that they can do whatever they want? Who cares if you're a better driver than she is?*

Peeking over at Deborah, who appeared unfazed, eyes closed with a faint smile adorning her lips, Joanna forced herself to gaze at the magnificent park scenery surrounding her as she struggled to regain the peace she had been feeling just moments before. *I am not going to let them ruin my day.* But, despite the peaceful atmosphere of stillness around her, Joanna couldn't remove the agitation from her brain. An unintended sigh escaped from her lips.

"You okay?" Deborah asked.

Another sigh. "Oh, yeah, sure."

"Are you okay?" Deborah repeated.

"I'm fine. It's just....I don't know. It's probably just that time of the month sneaking up on me."

"Things not going well with your grandma?" Deborah wondered.

"No, it's not that. Well, it's kind of that...and my uncle...and my mom." She drew in a long, deep breath. "Why do families have to be so complicated?"

"Yeah, families," Deborah quipped, "Can't live with 'em, can't kill 'em." Joanna managed a weak smile in response to Deborah's wittiness. "Hey, Jo, lighten up. You can't solve all the world's problems, you know."

"I know. It's just that I've spent so much together-time with Teddy and Grandma lately. And...I can't believe I'm even thinking this, but...I'm starting to see why my mom gets so exasperated with both of them. Everything is so....chaotic....all the time. I mean, I know everyone is entitled to live their lives the way they see fit, but...

"I mean, I'm cleaning and sorting, and packing and what do those two do? Yesterday, Teddy takes Grandma off to the flea market, and she comes home with an old crockpot, a muffin pan, and three cookie sheets that look like they've all spent time on the side of a road. And, the kicker is that Grandma already has so many pots and pans she doesn't even have enough space to store all of them in the kitchen. She keeps the excess under the bed in my room. Mom has told Teddy over and over again that he needs to stop letting Grandma buy things she doesn't need, but he never listens. He always claims that 'it's her money,' and does whatever the hell he wants.

"And, then if you confront him about it, he gives you this innocent look, like 'what did I do?' So, I usually don't bother. But the other day, I'd had it up to here. So, I let him have it, and, of course, Grandma is standing right behind me when I say, 'you know she's not going to live long enough to use all of this stuff, and she could probably use the cash to pay her bills and yours!'

"And, then Grandma says, 'You know, I'm not dead yet,' and shuffles off to her bedroom."

Staring out across the park, a tear trickled down Joanna's cheek. "Nice, right? What kind of granddaughter am I? Grandma has spent 79 years on this planet, and now I think I know what's best for her?" Joanna scrunched her face into a grimace then buried her face in her hands. "I'm starting to sound just like my mom."

"It could be worse," Deborah offered with a twinkle in her eye. "You could be starting to dress like her!" They giggled at the thought of Joanna in her mother's middle-aged business attire.

"Thanks for listening, Deb. You're a good friend."

Their remaining time together passed quickly. Reluctantly, Joanna glanced over her shoulder for one last look at Central Park as they waited for the light to change in front of the Plaza on Central Park South. They walked at a somewhat brisk pace back down 5th Avenue and passed Tiffany's, turning right on 56th. As they neared their restaurant destination, Joanna noticed a frantic Teddy pacing back and forth in front of Joe's Shanghai. When he spied Joanna and Deborah, he ran toward them, wringing his hands and looking more like a lost child than an adult well into his middle age.

The girls greeted Teddy, grabbing him by each arm and escorting him back toward the restaurant. "Hi, Teddy. Sorry if we're a bit late. Did you have a good day?" Joanna asked. "It was nice of you to meet us on the street, but I think we would have found the place on our own." She winked at Deborah.

"She's gone. She got away from me. It's not my fault," Teddy rambled on as he shifted back and forth from foot to foot, his face a pasty white.

Chapter 16

Joanna felt a stab of pain in her gut. "Oh, great. Just great. We're in New York frickin' City, and my grandmother is lost," she said.

"I just turned around for a second, and she was gone," Teddy whined, throwing his arms up in the air. "It's not my fault."

Realizing that there was no use in trying to establish what had actually happened, although suspecting that it really was Teddy's fault, Joanna asked, "Where is the last place you saw her?"

"Well, we were standing in front of Tiffany's and um...I needed...um, something to drink and so I, uh, looked around and...well, there's just no place to get anything on that street. So I...uh, walked around the corner and I was only gone for a minute, I swear! AND, I remember I told her to stay right there. When I came back, she wasn't there.

"I didn't know what to do so I pulled out your stupid map and came down here to Joe's Shanghai. I thought maybe she was hungry and came here on her own. But, when I got here, no one in the restaurant had seen her. So, I came outside, and there you were."

"Did you try her cell phone?" asked Joanna with a bit of condescension dripping from her voice.

"No. You know she doesn't know how to answer her cell phone and doesn't even keep it turned on. I don't even know why she has it," Teddy shot back.

"Ok, well, let's try that," she said, dialing Ruth's number. The phone rang several times, and then Beverly's primly recorded message came on "This is Ruth's cell phone. Please leave a message."

Joanna hung up without leaving a message. "Told ya'," came Teddy's pompous retort.

The evening sun twinkled against the building facades that lined West 56th Street. Joanna bowed her head and covered her face with her hands as she tried to think of what to do next, her heart sinking like the fading sun.

"Maybe we should call the police," offered Deborah half-heartedly.

Looking up at her friend, Joanna was temporarily blinded as a glint of sunlight caught the silver pendant on Deborah's necklace.

"I think I know where she is," Joanna shouted. She turned and hastily retraced her steps back down 56th with Deborah and Teddy trailing not far behind. Luckily, the traffic lights sensed the urgency in Joanna's journey and cooperated by turning green just as she reached each intersection. For such a short distance, it seemed to take forever, but soon they reached their destination: Tiffany's. Wasting no time, Joanna pushed herself through the revolving door and practically tripped over Ruth as she sat talking pleasantly with the hulking mass of a man who was employed as Tiffany's doorman/security guard.

"Grandma, thank goodness!" shrieked Joanna.

"Does this young lady belong to you, Ruth?" asked her newfound friend sweetly.

Joanna stared at him, caught off guard by his amiable demeanor. It contrasted oddly with the detached manner he had presented earlier in the day.

"Why yes, Ralph dear. This is my granddaughter," Ruth answered.

Standing to his full height, Ralph-dear glared down at Joanna. His security guard persona was in full force as he began to berate Joanna for her irresponsible behavior and the abandonment of her grandmother on the streets of New York City.

Teddy and Deborah arrived in time to hear the lecture, but neither of them came to Joanna's defense. In fact, at the sight of Ralph-dear, they both decided to exit the store and wait outside.

As Ralph continued with his diatribe against her, Joanna stood frozen, unable to move or to speak. Ruth gently touched Ralph's arm, and when he turned toward her, she said, "It's not her fault, dear. I just tripped. It sure doesn't pay to get old, don't you know."

"What? You tripped?" asked Joanna concerned and confused.

"Oh, just a little bit. Over there," Ruth grimaced as she offered a perplexed gaze toward the revolving door. "My word, they just spin so fast."

"Are you ok, Grandma?"

"Oh, I think she'll live," said Ralph, patting Ruth on the back and steadying her as she got to her feet. He smiled at Ruth, and then shot an accusatory glance at Joanna. "But, you really might want to take better care of this young lady."

"Okay, Officer, I will," Joanna agreed as Ralph-dear pushed the button for the handicapped door, allowing Ruth to exit the building without repeating her encounter with the revolving menace.

On the sidewalk outside, Teddy burst out, "Son of a bitch, Ma. You sure did have Joanna worried. I would never wander off like that."

"I got so tired while I was waiting for Teddy. I just went into Tiffany's to find a seat. That's when I met my new friend, Ralph, who was taking care of me," said Ruth.

Joanna felt the flush of anger on her face. "That's what Teddy should have been doing," she said under her breath. She shot a critical glare at Teddy.

"Whoa, whoa! I'm just here for the ride. Ma can take care of herself."

"No, she can't. That's why I had to come to New Jersey."

"Why's that, dear?"

"To take care of you."

"Oh, I thought it was the other way around."

"OO! Burn!" said Teddy.

Ruth took Teddy's arm. "Let's go eat."

Although Joanna knew her grandmother hadn't meant it, Ruth's words stung. Joanna felt a prickle on the back of her neck as she watched her uncle and grandmother walk off arm in arm toward the restaurant. A sharp elbow jab caught her attention.

"Come on Jo, let's go eat," said Deborah with a sympathetic smile.

As they walked back to the restaurant, Joanna contemplated just why her grandmother's comment was so disturbing. *She might as well just have said to me "Don't try to come in here and change* ***our*** *lives just to make* ***yourself*** *feel better." Why does this bother me so much?* she wondered.

A tug on her sleeve interrupted Joanna's thoughts. "We're here!" Deborah proclaimed as she pulled her through the door of Joe's Shanghai.

While waiting to be seated, Joanna tried to assuage her guilty conscience. *I just wanted a day with my friend. Is that a crime? I didn't even want Grandma to come with us. Grandma and Teddy just pushed their way into this trip. I just want Teddy to admit his part in Grandma's disappearance.*

As Joanna schemed, the waiter escorted them to their table and distributed menus.

"Grandma, when you were lost, did you call one of us?" asked Joanna.

"I didn't call, dear," said Ruth as she scanned the menu. "Ralph did."

"Ralph?... Oh! The scary man from Tiffany's?"

"Oh, he's not scary. His bark is worse than his bite. He asked me if I had a cell phone, and I said yes, my daughter Beverly had set me up with a phone, but I rarely make calls on it, don't you know. The buttons are so small that I can barely see them."

Joanna tried to keep Ruth on track. "So, Grandma, what happened?"

"Well, I took out the phone and asked him if he could see the buttons. He took that phone and just started to push those tiny things. He knew just what to do with it; I could see right away that he was a smart young man. Then, Ralph asked me who he should dial. I said to call Teddy, so he did, but he got your message, dear." Ruth turned to Teddy and patted his beefy hand.

Teddy pulled out his phone. "Yep. I have a missed call."

"Teddy, you were supposed to take care of Grandma. Nice job!" Joanna sneered, a sense of vindication pervading her comment.

"Well, damn, I bet I couldn't hear it on the street with all the noise."

Ruth steered the conversation back toward food. "I'm thinking we should order Lion's Head. It's been ages since I've had that."

"What happened next Grandma?" Joanna attempted to re-focus her.

"Well, Ralph asked me who else he should try. I said 'call Joanna,' so he did, but you didn't answer either."

"Ha!" Teddy blurted out. "You're no better, Miss Perfect."

Joanna pulled out her phone and found an unanswered call. Teddy was right; she really was no better.

"Did you give up after that?"

"Subgum."

"What?"

"Subgum Casserole. I definitely want to get some of that."

Joanna tried to get in Ruth's line of vision and lock eyes with her. "Grandma, did you see Teddy and me soon after you tried to call us?"

"Well, Ralph really wanted to get ahold of someone for me." She put down the menu and picked up the silverware at her place. She unrolled the napkin carefully placing the fork and knife on the table in front of her leaving room for a plate in between.

"Who did he call?" Joanna asked with a growing sense of unease.

"Well, the only other person I could think of was Beverly." Ruth looked up at Joanna. "I thought maybe she could get ahold of you or Teddy."

"Did you speak to her?"

Ruth nodded.

"What did you tell her?" Joanna asked, her voice rising.

"I asked if she knew how to get ahold of you. She said yes, but she didn't want to disturb your studying, Joanna." Ruth paused. "Dear, does your mother know that you are here?"

Joanna wanted to say, "No. She doesn't." But, she tried to see from Ruth's expression whether she was asking the question just as a test. Did Ruth already know the answer? Joanna swallowed hard and said, "Well, she knows that I'm in New Jersey."

Ruth seemed satisfied with Joanna's reply. "Well, that's good dear. She'll be here tomorrow. I'm so excited, aren't you?" She shot a knowing glance at Joanna and then resumed making plans for their dumpling dinner.

Joanna, on the other hand, found her thoughts racing. *Oh great, Mom is coming. She's going to ask me all kinds of questions about finals and grades, and I really don't want to talk about that with her. Oh, yikes, and she'll have a fit if Peanut is still here.*

Joanna was absent-mindedly chewing on her fingernails when a hand reached up and pulled her hand away from her mouth. "You'll spoil your appetite," said Deborah.

Chapter 17

Dinner was quickly devoured, but Joanna had been too preoccupied with the thought of Beverly's upcoming visit to really enjoy her meal. She hugged Deborah goodbye at the Port Authority and retrieved the car for the trip back home to Neshanic Station. On their journey home, Ruth talked non-stop about their glorious New York adventures while Teddy childishly proclaimed himself the winner of the non-existent soup dumpling-eating contest.

Normally, their incessant chitchat would have annoyed Joanna, but she was stuck on what to do with the dog before Beverly arrived the next day. Ruth loved Peanut. She would never agree to give him up. Teddy was keeping the energetic puppy at his house during the night, but during the day he had free run of Ruth's backyard and was often in her house. Joanna knew when Beverly came she would not be happy with the Peanut situation.

Joanna passed the turn off for Shady Oaks and thought of Lurena and Berta. Maybe one of them could keep Peanut during

Beverly's visit. Then she immediately realized there was no way that she could take Peanut near Berta — *a strong wind could knock her to the ground; a strong dog would flatten her.* Lurena was a possibility. Joanna asked Ruth, "Do you know if they allow pets at Shady Oaks?"

"Oh, poor Lurena. She had to find a new home for her little poodle when she moved. She was heartbroken, don't you know," Ruth shook her head. "Why do you ask, dear?"

Joanna cringed, "I was just thinking what good company a pet can be."

"That's really sweet of you to think of Lurena. She surely does get lonely." Ruth turned and reached a hand toward Teddy, who was now snoring in the backseat, completely unaware of the conversation. "I'm so blessed to have Teddy and Peanut so close by."

Ruth's answer confirmed what Joanna already knew; Ruth was not going to let go of Peanut easily, and she couldn't take Peanut to stay with a friend.

Joanna headed toward Teddy's house, driving a little too fast for the quiet residential street. She pulled into his driveway, put the car into neutral, and turned around. There slept Teddy—mouth agape, breathing heavily and apparently oblivious to their arrival. Reaching back, she tapped Teddy's knee. "Uncle Teddy, we're here," she said. Teddy snorted awake and wiped the drool from the side of his mouth.

"We're back already? That was fast."

"Yes. Time flies when you're sleeping. I'm going to take Grandma home and walk back with Peanut. I'll see you in about half an hour. Okay?"

Teddy grunted as he got out of the car, so Joanna wasn't really sure about what he had comprehended.

Once he was clear of the car, she backed out of the driveway and continued on to Ruth's house. She parked the car in Ruth's driveway and quickly slipped out of the driver's seat and trotted over to help Ruth out of the car. Joanna knew that once she had Ruth settled into her favorite chair in the living room, she could turn her attention to Peanut. She suddenly shuddered at the thought of turning mob enforcer for her mother. *Am I going to take care of Peanut or "take care" of Peanut?*

Steadying Ruth with one hand on the back stoop, Joanna turned the key in the lock and pushed against the door. Countering Joanna's effort from the inside was a whining, tail-wagging Peanut, pressing his wiggling body against the door. Joanna pushed harder on the door, inching it open despite the 80-pound puppy working to get to Ruth by scratching his way through the door.

Once Joanna successfully wrestled the door open, Peanut lunged up onto Ruth, covering her with slobbery kisses, nearly knocking her to the ground. Ruth patted Peanut lovingly, then shuffled off with him to the living room.

After getting Ruth settled with a cup of tea and the TV remote, Joanna grabbed Peanut's leash, clipped it to the dog's collar, and rushed out the door.

As Joanna and Peanut walked down the street, Peanut alternately trailed behind and bolted ahead, sniffing trees and chasing squirrels. Joanna, trying to walk briskly, felt annoyed by the jerk on the leash that she felt every few feet as Peanut turned toward another distraction. Joanna envied that he didn't seem to have a care in the world.

Continuing down the street, a pattern began to emerge. When Peanut approached a tree, Joanna knew that he would go over to it and sniff. Peanut seemed to know he could investigate as far away from her as the leash would allow. He would strain against it until Joanna tugged; then he would return to the sidewalk and continue happily along, anticipating the next tree. Gradually, Joanna realized that Peanut was really the one in control. When a tree required olfactory investigation, he would simply stand his ground, causing Joanna to stop for a moment, allowing him a few more seconds before yielding to the inevitable tug of the leash. "Oh, I see how it is. You hold your ground and get what you want. Is that your secret?" Joanna smiled down at Peanut. Then, her brow furrowing, she said. "Hmmm... if only it was that simple with Mom."

Once they had completed the circle around the neighborhood, Joanna headed back toward Teddy's to hide Peanut away until the coast was clear and Beverly had come and gone.

As Joanna approached the house, she saw Teddy sitting on his back step. Unclipping Peanut's leash, she gave the large puppy a pat on the head and said, "Be good."

"Hi Boy," said Teddy, putting down his beer and leaning forward to pet Peanut on the head. "Owww…My back is hurting something fierce from all that walking today. Grab Peanut's food from the garage, would you?" Joanna suppressed the desire to point out that the lack of activity in Teddy's normal everyday life was more likely to blame.

As she reached for the puppy chow, she heard a car door slam and loud chortling in the driveway. Teddy called out, "Dudes!" A cacophony of door slams and stomping feet followed as the 'dudes' arrived in Teddy's driveway. The guys appeared to be oblivious to Joanna's presence until she interrupted them by introducing herself and offering her hand to the closest 'dude.'

"Hi, I'm Joanna." Her introduction was greeted by stunned silence, and she stood with her un-received right hand hanging in mid-air.

Feeling awkward, Joanna reminded herself that these were Nutty Uncle Teddy's friends. Then, to her surprise, one of them took Joanna's still outstretched hand and pressed it to his heart.

"It is a great pleasure to make your acquaintance, lovely lady," he said in his best imitation of 19th century chivalry.

Joanna grimaced at him. "Nice to…meet…you, too," she said haltingly as she tried to withdraw her hand.

Teddy and the other two guys just stared as the overly-friendly one tried to make his move on Joanna. Still clutching her hand, he changed from gentleman-speak to Jersey gibberish. "Well, now, baby," he ogled her up and down. "How you doin'?" He moved in uncomfortably close to her.

Frazzled and disgusted by the incident, she wiggled her hand free and backed away to a safe distance.

"Okay, knock it off, Percy. That's my niece," Teddy finally said in her defense. "Besides you're 20 years older than she is…and you have a girlfriend."

The other two sniggered.

"Cut it out, Steve and Spike," Teddy reprimanded.

"I'm just happy that there's less competition," Steve winked, prompting guffaws from all four guys.

These guys are more 'crude' than 'dude.' Joanna thought, desperately wanting to get away. She strategized her escape that would involve squeezing past a lot of middle-aged flab. When a small gap appeared in the buffoonery, she forced her way through the slightly, open path. Nearly free, it suddenly dawned on her that she might just get these morons to help her. She took a deep breath and turned back to say, "Hey, would you guys be willing to help out my grandma by moving some things out to the curb?"

The laughter stopped and Percy said, "Sure! Anything for Mrs. Lathrop."

The other guys all nodded. Joanna was stunned. She never expected them to be so willing.

"There's only one condition," added Steve.

Dang it! thought Joanna. *There's always a catch.*

"We're going to need some beer," said Steve.

Joanna felt a rush of relief. "Okay. It's a deal. Come over tomorrow morning about 10:00, and we'll get to work." She quickly slipped away before they had a chance to renege

Chapter 18

As soon as she was a safe distance from Teddy and the 'dudes,' Joanna savored the first bit of quiet since the action-packed, lose-your-grandmother-in-the-Big-Apple trip. Peanut had been taken care of, at least temporarily, and she had convinced Teddy and his friends to remove some of the junk at Grandma's for the mere promise of a couple of beers. *They may be childish and immature, but at least they'll be able to move some of that crap out of the house. Am I good or what?* But her moment of triumph was short lived. *Now all I have to do is deal with Mom.* Shaking her head, she cringed. *Who am I kidding? I came out here thinking I that I could save the day, but now what I really have to do is convince Beverly that I have.*

Back in Ruth's kitchen, Joanna's anxiety followed her as she hollered for her grandmother.

"I'm in here, dear," came Ruth's reply.

Absentmindedly chewing her fingernails, Joanna followed Ruth's voice into the living room and was met by her grandmother's sincere gaze. "You've been awfully quiet since we left New York, Sweetie. What's up?"

"Oh, I don't know," Joanna answered as she spat a hangnail across the room. "Just a lot on my mind I guess."

Satisfied with Joanna's noncommittal answer, Ruth returned to perusing the *TV Guide.*

What is up with me? Joanna wondered as she pondered Ruth's question. *How come whatever I do is never good enough?*

Feeling her mother's strangle hold on her psyche tighten, Joanna began a conversation with Beverly in her head. *Yeah, Mom I screwed up again. The trip to New York was just another episode of poor judgment on my part. Thanks for noticing.*

Joanna could just hear Beverly's holier-than-thou reply, "Don't you have a bagful of regrets."

Suddenly Ruth suggested, "Hey, I know what let's do! *North by Northwest* is on tonight."

"I don't know if I feel like it." Joanna droned.

"But it's Cary Grant!"

"I don't deserve Cary Grant after the day I've had."

"Well, sweetie, don't let your bag get too full of regrets."

So, that's how that expression goes. It sounds a lot different when mom says it.

When Joanna didn't respond, Ruth swayed in her chair three times before rising and hobbling toward the kitchen. "I know what will take your mind off your troubles. Come on." Ruth grabbed Joanna's hand and ushered her to the sink. "We have just enough time to wash those breakfast dishes before we settle in."

Joanna stood next to Ruth at the sink, watching her squeeze Ivory dish soap under the running water as the sink filled. Joanna's mind was numb; her feeling of inadequacy was stifling. She started to cry, her tears splashing into the soapy dishwater.

Lost in her thoughts and self-pity, Joanna jumped as Ruth's hug enveloped her from behind. "Are you okay, Joanna?" Ruth asked cautiously.

Without turning around, Joanna nodded her head, trying not to breathe in and give away her tears and stuffed up nose. Joanna saw a tear fall gracefully onto Ruth's wrist just below her watch and then felt her grandmother's embrace tighten around her.

"Whatever it is, my sweet. It can't be all that bad," Ruth offered.

Joanna turned to face Ruth and leaned her head down onto Ruth's shoulder. Almost a foot taller than her grandmother, Joanna leaned down awkwardly. Despite the unbalanced stance, the love she felt in Ruth's grip comforted her, and she held on for what seemed like too long. But Ruth's hug never waivered: she never got antsy, never sighed, never said, "C'mon get over yourself," all the things she had come to expect from her mother when she needed comfort.

Ruth stood there stroking her adult granddaughter's hair and waited for Joanna to make the first move. Only when the sink water looked close to overflowing did Ruth lean over to turn off the tap.

"Oh, Grandma," Joanna sighed. "Why can't I be more like you?"

"Because then you wouldn't be you," Ruth countered.

"Yeah, but maybe that would be a good thing. Just like *It's a Wonderful Life* – maybe it would have been better if I had never been born."

"But, you remember how that one comes out, right?" Ruth cradled Joanna's chin, brushed the hair out of her face, and gently placed a kiss on her tear stained-cheek.

"Yeah, I know."

"Did I ever tell you 'bout the time my daddy got to feeling blue?" Ruth asked as she grabbed the dishrag and started to wash.

Joanna stood beside her, ready to dry the first clean plate that Ruth handed to her.

"Well, it was just after my parents were first married—just after the stock market crashed. My daddy hated the farm, but they'd lost everything. No money, no house, and a baby—me, on the way. They had no choice; they moved back to the farm, to live with his parents, my grandparents.

"Well, don't you know, everything on that farm was in need of a face lift, but there was food and a roof over their heads. He tried to get work, but there was nothing available. Every day, momma could see Daddy getting more and more depressed. One night when he didn't come in from the barn, she got worried and went out looking for him. She found him sitting on a stool holding a noose. 'Guess you'd be better off without me,' he said.

"Well, I'm here to tell you," Ruth stopped washing and turned to face Joanna. "My momma just looked down at her belly, then back at him, and hollered, 'how could you think such a thing?'"

"What happened? He didn't…"

"No, no he didn't. He used to tell me about it when I got to feeling blue about something or other. He'd say, 'Ain't nothin' so bad it can't be fixed.' And, he's right you know. Whatever's going on in that head of yours, it will get better. And, you'll be glad again. I've got to say, your presence here has really been a blessing for me this week. And, I don't just mean you taking care of me. I mean you."

Joanna smiled, feeling very loved.

Ruth dropped the dishrag and led Joanna toward the living room. "Let's leave these dishes to soak. Cary Grant should be holding the knife at the UN about now."

Chapter 19

Joanna woke with a feeling of anticipation, mixed with anxiety, like she had forgotten something. She had other things on her mind, but she hadn't forgotten that it was Thanksgiving. Beverly would be arriving at noon, so the mass of Ruth's donate-able items would need to be moved outside to be ready for pick-up on Friday.

Standing in front of the pile around the piano, she said, "Wow, this is going to be a big job!" Hands on hips, she bit her lower lip and wondered, *I know I can't do it without them, but will having Teddy and his friends over to "help" really be helpful?*

Maybe I need to remind Teddy. A quick text took care of that, but the feeling that she had overlooked something remained.

What did I forget? The beer? Can't forget that! A quick check in the fridge confirmed that there was a 12-pack handy. But something was still not right.

Walking toward the living room, a feeling of dread sat in her stomach as she realized she had not filled Ruth in on her plan, or even asked her permission to donate her things.

Once in the living room, Joanna saw her chance as Ruth was readying herself for Euchre Day with her girlfriends at Shady Oaks. They had been "playing" Euchre for years, rotating the destination of their weekly game from one house to another. But, as her friends began passing on or taking up residence at the "old folk's home," their weekly card date had moved to Shady Oaks and had evolved into a full day of socializing with a few rounds of Euchre thrown in - if they felt like it. Even though the card game was optional, they never missed getting together on Thursday mornings, even on major holidays.

"Morning, Grandma," Joanna began cautiously, "I was just wondering if I remembered to tell you…the people who take donations will come and pick up all of the items we've been putting aside. You know, all of that stuff we piled in the back bedroom and also the stuff piled around the piano?"

Ruth seemed distracted as she fidgeted with her jacket, trying, without success, to get her arm into the inside-out sleeve as she peered anxiously out the front door. "I wonder what's keeping Teddy this morning," Ruth said more to herself than to Joanna. It was Teddy's job to transport Ruth to Shady Oaks, but he was, not surprisingly Joanna noted, nowhere to be found.

Joanna reached over to help Ruth with her jacket. "Is that okay with you, Grandma?"

Bundled up and holding her pocketbook, Ruth seemed quick to agree with Joanna as she continued to gaze restlessly out the front door. "Yes, Dear, that's fine. Never do get much use out of that piano anymore."

Joanna's eyes brightened. *I think I just got permission to donate the piano, too!*

Suddenly, the tension in Ruth's face melted away, and she smiled as Teddy entered the house. "There you are, my sugar boy. Come on, times a-wastin'."

Teddy scratched his head and grunted something indistinguishable. Ruth started to respond, but Joanna was quick to escort her grandmother to the car, buckle her in, and close the door before Ruth could change her mind about the donation.

As Teddy sauntered around the car, Joanna abruptly grabbed his arm and said, "Remember to pick up your buddies on the way back so we can get to work."

Teddy pulled his arm back and gave her a mock salute. "Yes, ma'am!"

Joanna rolled her eyes and shot back, "Just get back here to give me a hand, okay?"

As she returned to the living room, surveying the piles, she wondered outloud, "What have I gotten myself into?" She pictured Teddy's peculiar friends and hoped they would actually do some work *and* leave quickly. She sank down into Grandpa's patched recliner and reminded herself of her mission to help her grandmother. *You volunteered for this.*

Nudging the nearest pile with her foot, she could hear Grandpa saying one of his infamous motivational phases, "Hop to it, bunny rabbit!" She groaned, smiled at the memory, and then hopped up. Hefting the nearest box and grabbing two bags on her way to the front door, she made her way out and to the curb. Forty-five minutes later, after multiple, mindless trips outside, she had exposed the dreadful state of the piano.

Standing wearily on its four tiny metal wheels, it appeared to sag and moan under its own bulk. Joanna remembered her fascination with it as a child. She would plunk at the keys, producing a honky-tonk melody, but she couldn't actually recall ever hearing Ruth play a tune on it.

One time when Joanna asked her grandmother why it was there, Ruth had answered with a far off look in her eye, "Oh, it was the first brand-new thing your grandfather and I bought with our own hard-earned money when we set up housekeeping. Isn't it just the most beautiful thing you have ever seen?"

Looking at the forlorn instrument, Joanna honestly could not fathom how the word 'beautiful' could be associated with such a dilapidated monstrosity. Joanna opened the keyboard lid and struck what should have been middle C. "THUD, THUD, THUD." Nothing musical left here, she thought. *If Teddy would ever get back, we can move you to the curb, too.*

On Joanna's next trip outside, she noted that Teddy had returned with the "dudes."

"Finally," she said under her breath. Before they could goof-off, Joanna herded them toward the massive upright piano that sat crammed into the over-crowded living room, encroaching on the kitchen doorway

"You want us to move that thing?" hollered Steve. "What are you – crazy or sumthin'?"

"Are you trying to kill us?" Teddy chimed in as he massaged and stretched his low back.

Percy sidled up to Joanna. "I'll help you. Then you, can help me, if you know what I mean." He reached over to put his arm around her shoulders.

Fuming, Joanna ducked to avoid Percy's affection and commanded, "Everyone. Grab a corner. Let's move!" Amazingly, the guys gathered around the piano. "Ok, now push it over to the front door," she barked at them like an irritated drill sergeant.

Despite a lack of any enthusiasm, the group reluctantly obeyed. Struggling against the piano's bulk, they attempted to push, and then pull, it toward the door. The piano's wheels, obviously rusted tight over time, stubbornly refused to roll.

"You can do it, guys! Just think of the appetite you'll work up for your Thanksgiving dinner tonight!" Joanna urged the guys on while they huffed and puffed and cussed.

Suddenly, the piano lurched a couple inches forward and then stopped abruptly. The front door was a mere 10 feet from the piano's original resting place, but moving it across the living room was proving to be an exhausting task. Sweating and wheezing, Teddy turned toward Joanna and opened his mouth to voice a complaint.

"Don't even think about it," Joanna warned.

Teddy closed his mouth, took in a deep breath, and then braced himself for another push against the reluctant target. The piano made a screeching sound as it resisted further movement across the floor but then jumped forward another few inches. Watching their futile efforts, Joanna contemplated the wisdom of her decision to recruit physically-unfit, middle-aged men for this task. *I hope one of them doesn't have a heart attack.*

Panting with exhaustion, Percy and Spike fell to their knees; Teddy and Steve collapsed in a heap on the sofa. However, when Joanna agreed to reward their efforts with a beer, they all made a miraculous recovery. "But just one," she warned.

The guys cheered in unison. As Joanna went into the kitchen to grab the beverages, she could hear their childish boasting and insults as they compared the size of their biceps and debated who had worked the hardest. Each of them assured the others that without his hulking masculinity the task of hauling a piano "across the living room" would have been impossible. In fact, each claimed that his abilities had made the difference.

"A piece of cake," boasted Teddy.

"A breeze," bragged Percy.

"A walk in the park," crowed Spike.

"A real ball-buster," quipped Steve. Joanna smiled to herself as she reasoned that ball-busting would actually have meant that Steve's contribution was not that helpful, but it didn't matter to the rest of the guys. They were lost in laughter as she made her way back to them.

Her distribution of the bottles of Bud Lite promoted a few groans at the notion of how lite beer might diminish their manliness. But, when Joanna pulled the bottle opener from her pocket and opened her own brew, it didn't take the rest of them long to follow suit. Spike was so eager to partake of his reward that he raised his bottle to his mouth, deftly opening it with his teeth, spitting the cap out onto the floor and downing his beer in six long tugs. Streams of the beverage oozed down his chin as he slammed his empty bottle down on the floor next to the piano and proceeded to belch the alphabet. His juvenile audience cheered and tried to compete, but their burps, while disgusting, could not compare.

Joanna couldn't believe what she was seeing and hearing. These guys seemed to be straight out of the movie *Animal House.* Joanna wondered, *How can grown men act so much like 18-year-old frat boys?* But then, she remembered that these were Nutty Uncle Teddy's friends. "It figures," she said under her breath.

Alcohol consumption seemed to do a lot for the guys' morale. They bantered back and forth, resuming their pre-adolescent personas. Joanna fed into their egos by complimenting them.

"You guys were great! Northwest Vanlines look out!" she praised them. Her tactic seemed to be working as the men continued to argue good-naturedly amongst themselves about who had exerted the most energy.

After what Joanna deemed an appropriate amount of time for them to have rested and regained their strength, she announced, "Alright then, my most excellent movers, back to work it is."

The silliness ceased abruptly as the guys' miserable moans hung forlornly in the air. Teddy massaged his back again. Steve rubbed a knee. Spike groaned as he attempted to lift himself from the floor.

"I'd love to help you darlin'," Percy offered, "but Doc says I ain't 'posed to do any liftin' on account of my hernia." Percy had an apologetic look in his eye that almost convinced Joanna of his sincerity until he reached for his fly and added, "If you don't believe me, you can feel it for yourself, sugar."

The guys howled with laughter. Joanna hung her head, shook it, and tried to ignore their behavior. "C'mon guys. This piano's not going to walk outside by itself," she sighed, trying to remain positive.

"It might as well," Steve replied defiantly. "I couldn't walk if my life depended on it right now." He stared at her with a surly look.

"Yeah, it has feet," Teddy quipped. "Why don't you nag at it like you've been nagging at us? See if you can get it to walk itself out to the curb." He burst into laughter, starting yet another round of snickers and snide comments from Percy and Steve.

Spike thought for a moment and then added with sincere, child-like enthusiasm, "I'd like to see that."

"Look," Joanna tried again struggling to contain her rising temper. "I just need you guys to get the piano outside, and then you can stretch out on the couch with another cold beer."

"No way," resisted Percy. "But you and I can sit on the couch and get to know each other better." He winked at Joanna prompting laughter from the other 'dudes.'

"When are you guys going to grow up?" Joanna queried.

Teddy and his cronies ignored her as their childish behavior continued.

What was I thinking when I recruited these guys? The frustration with Teddy and his friends that had been welling up inside of Joanna all day suddenly exploded. "Alright guys, I've had it up to here!" Joanna hollered waving her hand above her head to indicate to just where she was fed up. The guys, now absorbed in more childish banter about their sexual prowess, paid her no attention. She drew in a deep breath and tried again. "Come on you guys. I gave you beer, and there's more where that came from," she pleaded.

The mention of beer grabbed the attention of her male counterparts. They stopped laughing and turned to look at her. "Sure, I'll take one, darlin'," said Percy.

"Me too," added Steve while Spike nodded his head in agreement.

"Yeah, but not that watered-down lite crap. Run out and get us some real beer," Teddy commanded.

That really was it. She grabbed the nearest thing to her, which happened to be the long handled axe resting behind the front door. The axe had significant weight; however, Joanna wielded it over her head like a feather. Nevertheless, despite her fierce stance, her angry display only served to produce more adolescent guffaws and demands for real beer. Detecting that her threat was having less than its intended effect, she swung the axe wildly about, allowing its weight to determine its path. It came to rest, with an off-key musical thud, in the keyboard of Ruth's piano. Several ivories sailed through the air, and the wooden keyboard cover slammed shut at a skewed angle over the axe blade. That action silenced the laughter and drew a few inhales of fear from the guys, but Joanna hardly noticed. The accidental blow felt invigorating as it allowed her pent up feelings to release. She wiggled the axe-blade free and continued to hack away at the piano, taking out her frustrations with each successive swing.

Smack! To Teddy and his friends. Kapow! To her inablity to really help her grandmother. Whack! To her less than stellar performance at school. Slam! To her mother's constant dissatisfaction with her. Crack! To the guilt at the lies she told her dad. Blow after blow, Joanna chopped away at the defenseless instrument. Severed pieces of splintered wood fell at her feet. Some spewed wildly around the room. All of her frustrations, all of her inadequacies, all of her inabilities poured forth from the weapon in her hand until all that remained of her grandmother's piano was the massive metal frame surrounded by kindling and mangled piano strings. Exhausted, Joanna laid the axe on the ground and surveyed her handiwork.

She glanced over at Teddy and the guys who appeared to be huddled together. They eyed her fearfully. Spike wore a horrified grimace. Without saying a word, Joanna marched into the kitchen and returned moments later holding an open beer; the axe slung carelessly over her shoulder. She proceeded to guzzle her brew, belch loudly, and toss the empty bottle into the trashcan from 3-point range. “C'mon guys, let's see if you can outdo that one!”

The fear in the room was palpable. The guys cowered together, clutching at each other for protection. Moving silently toward the door, but keeping their eyes fixed on Joanna and her large axe, they attempted to escape.

“OH. NO. YOU. DON’T! Nobody’s going anywhere until this piano is outside where it belongs!”

Stunned, the four men queried each other silently, *stay or bolt?* With a turn of his head and a pointed look, Teddy reminded the group of the large weapon in Joanna’s hand. Their attitudes changed to an uneasy submission as they moved en masse toward the wreckage, systematically removing the remains.

Obediently the guys lugged and tugged the soundboard outside. After haphazardly piling the piano kindling in and around the garbage can in the garage, Teddy glanced toward the house and motioned to the car in the driveway. The guys nodded in understanding, and the group slunk nervously toward the escape vehicle. Joanna walked out onto the sidewalk with an armload of bags and saw the car inching out of the driveway. Although inwardly' she was relieved they were leaving, she turned and muttered, "Quitters!"

As Teddy maneuvered the car toward the street, Joanna suddenly remembered that Teddy needed to retrieve Ruth from Shady Oaks. With sarcasm dripping from her tongue, she yelled, "Thanks for saying goodbye and, by the way, don't forget to get Grandma!" Kicking up gravel as it accelerated away, the carload of 'dudes' fled off down Olive Lane.

Chapter 20

Joanna, feeling a sense of empowerment, headed back into the house and surveyed her work. *Ah! A new sense of space.* Her gaze swept over the new emptiness, landing on the spot that the ill-fated piano had so recently occupied. With a sense of smugness and the realization that she would no longer be stubbing her toe as she attempted to enter the kitchen, she kicked off her shoes and walked over to stand on the previously piano-protected area. Smiling to herself, she looked down and said to her toes, "I did this for you, little piggies."

But, then her eyes were instantly drawn to the contrast between the newly visible rectangle of clean carpet and the well-trodden, grungy shag that covered the rest of the living room and ran sadly down the hallway to the bedrooms. "Did I really make you walk on that?" she asked her feet as she poked at the dirty carpet with the toes of her right foot. "Oww," she screamed as a splintered remnant of piano lodged itself in her big toe. She hopped into the kitchen and over to a chair to inspect her wound. Attempting to grab the splinter with her fingernails, she realized that the doctor in the ER was right—she needed to stop biting her nails.

Having nothing but stubs for fingernails, she decided she needed tweezers. She hobbled over to the junk drawer in the kitchen, knowing that she'd be able to find exactly what she was looking for, but it wouldn't open. She tugged at the knob which jostled the contents of the drawer just enough to allow her to reach in and find what was impeding its opening. It was a Rubik's Cube. Dislodging it, she wondered if it was the one she lost when she was 10. She set it aside and dug through the tangled mess in the drawer, finding three different kinds of tweezers. Luckily, she also found a Band-aid and Bactine. Scooping up the least-rusted pair of tweezers, she set to work on extracting her splinter.

After a quick tug with the tweezers, a squirt of Bactine, and successfully applying the ancient Band-aid, she eagerly snatched up the worn Rubik's Cube. Slowly turning it over in her hands, she recalled her acumen with the Cube in her younger days, and then delighted in solving it behind her back and with one eye closed. "Damn, I am a axe-wielding, Rubik's Cube-solving, Bee-otch!"

Her euphoria, however, was short-lived as she glanced at the scene unfolding in the front yard. First, she noticed Teddy's car pull into the driveway. All four of the guys exited the car and headed off down the sidewalk, leaving Ruth to get out of the car by herself.

"Nice way to help your mother, Uncle Teddy," she mumbled to herself, knowing full well he couldn't hear her. Although she recognized that she should jump up and help Ruth out of the car, her puzzle solving addiction pulled her back in.

"Yes!" Joanna exclaimed as she completed the red side. But her satisfaction was short lived as she was distracted by a scrapping sound from outside. She glanced up to see her grandmother laboriously dragging a trash bag full of who-knows-what up the sidewalk from the pile on the curb.

At first, Joanna marveled at her grandmother's stamina for such a physical task. "How can such a small woman with a bum leg do that?" Joanna wondered aloud to herself. Then, when she saw Ruth pause at the front steps, a flash of horror shot through Joanna as she realized that her grandmother was contemplating how she was going to carry her treasure-load up the steps and back into the house.

Just then, a taxicab pulled up at the foot of the driveway. Joanna watched in slow motion as her mother emerged from the car and tipped the driver who had just extracted her luggage from the trunk. Beverly picked up her suitcase, and then homed in on her elderly mother who was attempting to drag a bulging trash bag up the front step.

There was a part of Joanna that urged herself to make an immediate dash out of the house and intervene. But, watching the surreal scene that was unfolding outside kept Joanna from leaving her vantage point in the safety of the house.

As Beverly strutted up the front walk in her wrinkle-free suit and heels, looking as if she was ready to show a house rather than having just traveled across the country, Joanna heard her shriek, "Mother!" Beverly unhanded her suitcase and grabbed the trash bag from Ruth. "What are you doing?"

She tottered around in her place to greet Beverly with outstretched arms. "Well, hello sweetie." Ruth shuffled toward her daughter in anticipation of an embrace.

But instead of a hug, Beverly gave Ruth a quick peck on the cheek and demanded, "Where is Joanna?"

"Oh, she's in the house," Ruth responded.

Beverly huffed in frustration, "I suppose Joanna is off sulking somewhere. She should know better than to let her grandmother lift heavy loads."

Beverly sighed as she reached up to smooth a curl of her hair that had suddenly swung out of place and into her line of vision.

In disbelief, Joanna watched the disjointed interchange between her mother and her grandmother. "*It's* really going to hit the fan now." Joanna took a deep breath as she headed toward the front door.

Emerging from the house, Joanna reached for the trash bag. "Here, I'll take that to the curb for you, Grandma."

"No, dear. I'm taking that back into the house."

Disregarding Ruth's comment, Joanna turned toward the street. Before she could take a step, she found herself on the receiving end of an obligatory air-kiss-on-the-cheek.

"Hello Joanna," said Beverly, reaching over to push Joanna's hair away from her face.

Trying to sound upbeat, Joanna said, "Hi Mom!"

"What prompted your change of plans? I expected you to be with your father for Thanksgiving."

If things weren't already awkward enough, suddenly out of the corner of her eye, Joanna saw Peanut pulling her rotund uncle down the sidewalk toward the house. Teddy's fan club of Spike, Percy, and Steve were in tow behind them. With Beverly facing the house, Joanna hoped that her mother had not seen "that damn dog" yet. Joanna tried to wave them off, but as soon as Peanut saw her, he bolted toward the house. Then, before anyone could do anything about it, Joanna saw Peanut zero in on Beverly.

"No!" Joanna yelled out, as she tugged at her mother's arm.

Beverly jumped. "Joanna! Really?"

With a tense smile and false cheer, Joanna tried to cover for her outburst, "Nope! I'm here, Mom! Right here in New Jersey." Pulling her mother toward the door, Joanna tried to maneuver Beverly into the house before the large puppy made it to the front yard. But, Peanut bounded quickly across the yard, barking and wagging his tail, his leash bouncing joyfully along behind.

Turning, Beverly gasped and clutched at her chest at the sight of the over-zealous canine barreling toward her. No words escaped from her lips, but the disdain she felt toward Peanut was apparent from the look of disgust on her face.

Horrified, Joanna patted at her knees and beckoned, "Here, Peanut," in a voice that sounded more frantic than endearing.

Ruth's eyes lit up in delight as she saw her gregarious pet. "There's my good boy. Here Pea-pea," Ruth giggled and held out her hand.

Normally, Peanut loved the attention Ruth and Joanna showered on him and would probably have bounded over to them when called. But, adding a newcomer to the mix always caused the large puppy to lose all sense of loyalty, and become eagerly intent on greeting the new person— apparently his self-proclaimed calling in life. And so, fixating on Beverly, the fresh face in the crowd, Peanut jumped up on his hind legs, placed his forelegs on Beverly's shoulders, and commenced in enthusiastically licking her face. Beverly froze, her whole body stiffening. Ruth cackled in delight at the bonding ritual, while Joanna struggled to contain Peanut in all his excitement.

After what seemed like an eternity to Joanna, she managed to wrestle Peanut away from her mother. Struggling to maintain her grip on Peanut, Joanna peered over to assess Beverly's condition and caught sight of Teddy and his friends as they tried to make their escape in Teddy's vehicle. Annoyed at the situation, in general, and furious at Teddy's lack of responsible behavior in particular, Joanna yelled, "Hey, where do you think you're going!"

Teddy, holding the open car door, hesitatingly turned, then eased the car door shut.

"Hey, Sis!" hollered Teddy, as he started toward the chaos. "Welcome to New Jersey!"

To Joanna, it appeared as though Teddy was coming to her aid, but instead, he approached Beverly, grabbing the collar of her white blouse, and said, "Thanks for wearing…pause for effect… a new jersey..." another pause and a snicker "....in the latest Peanut print!"

The guys went wild. If looks could have killed, Beverly's piercingly, irate gaze aimed directly at them would have done the job.

"Yeah, Bevie, you look..." Percy paused, trying to stifle his own delight,"....'dog gone' delicious."

More howling from Teddy's gang ensued. Beverly inhaled slowly and methodically. Joanna could tell her mother was trying to control her rage, because Joanna had witnessed this all too often during her childhood when Beverly was trying to turn around a real estate deal about to go bad.

"Teddy," Beverly seethed through her clenched teeth. Slowly, she drew in a second breath as she prepared her next comment. "What.... is.... that.... damn.... dog.... still.... doing.... here?"

The boys were silent. Percy, Spike, and Steve looked to Teddy for guidance, not quite sure whether fun time was over or not.

Teddy scanned the yard. "I'm afraid I don't know what you mean, sis." He paused, feigning confusion, then turned toward his audience for the punch line. "There's no beaver here that I can see." Percy, Spike, and Steve looked dazed, not understanding if Teddy was making a joke or had suddenly turned serious. Not receiving the comedic response he had hoped for from his pals, Teddy explained.

"You know, a beaver builds dams, get it?" Still nothing. "Guys, come on. You're killing me. ...a DAM dog... 'Dam' without an 'N,' get it?" Teddy chuckled at his own play on words that prompted a tittering of guffaws from the guys. Joanna could tell that they really didn't understand the play on words, but in their defense, she acknowledged it was a pretty bad pun. But that was part of Teddy's charm, or at least his persona, and she caught herself smiling despite the gravity of the situation. That brief respite from the tension ended all too quickly, however, when Joanna glanced at her mother and noted a change in her demeanor, although not a change for the better.

Beverly, still disheveled, had managed to brush off some of Peanut's grime. She stood erect, appearing taller than her 5 foot 4 in-heels height. Her pale cheeks had turned bright crimson; even her hands seemed to glow red. If ever there was a time for the use of the phrase, 'steam coming out of your ears,' this would have been it, and Joanna even caught herself worrying about her mother's health. *I hope she remembered to take her blood pressure medicine today.*

"Very funny, Ted," Beverly began.

The use of the adult version of his name caught the group's attention. *No one calls him Ted*, Joanna gasped, and the rest of group inhaled a faint, yet distinct, breath in anticipation of what was to come.

Beverly continued in a sarcastic deadpan. "Don't give up your day job... Oh wait, that's right. You don't have a day job, do you?"

Percy started to laugh, but caught himself as he realized no one else was joining in.

Joanna glanced from her mother to Teddy. Beverly stood with a smug expression on her face. *Score one for Mom*, Joanna made a mental note.

"Well, at least I care about my family, unlike some people here," Teddy countered. Percy's brow furled, looking worried.

Surely Percy doesn't think that Teddy was referring to him, Joanna wondered. But, Joanna noticed Percy's relief when he must have deduced that Teddy's comment was aimed at Beverly instead.

"Care about your family?" queried Beverly. "Then why is that damn dog still here?" Percy started to snicker again, but stifled himself as the siblings' spat continued.

"Ma loves Peanut, and Peanut loves Ma," Teddy whined. Joanna tightened her grip on Peanut as he made an effort to lunge at the sound of his name. "They look out for each other, but then that's something you wouldn't know anything about. The only person you take responsibility for is yourself."

"Oh, please, little brother, you don't know the first thing about taking responsibility." Beverly's remark dripped with superiority. Joanna watched their exchange, trying to decide with whom she should side. Beverly had a point about Teddy. He was goofy and irresponsible, but Joanna didn't understand her mother's need to be so callous. It was easy to kindheartedly out-logic Teddy. *Or, was it*, she wondered as she recalled the guys' behavior that had caused her to smash Ruth's piano to bits. But, Joanna curbed her inner struggle when she heard Teddy's next comment.

"Well, if I had a daughter at least I would know where she was." Teddy's revelation was delivered haughtily enough to silence the entire group. Even Peanut sensed the seriousness of the situation as he lay down and let out a throaty doggy-sigh.

"I know exactly where my daughter is."

"Children!" Ruth stomped her good foot. "That's neither here nor there." Ruth's tone stunned Joanna. She had never heard such intensity in Ruth's voice before, and from Beverly's contrite look, it was possible she hadn't either. "I will not have the two of you fighting. Both of you, in the house now!"

Teddy and his pals attempted to make their exit, backing away slowly toward the sidewalk as Ruth continued to reprimand her children. Grabbing Teddy by a clump of hair, she shuttled him away like a bad schoolboy being taken to the principal's office. "We're going to sit at the table and work this out no matter how long it takes!"

When Ruth entered the living room, she gasped. "Where is my piano!?"

Joanna tried to squeeze between Teddy and the doorway, and then make a beeline for the back bedroom, but Ruth grabbed Joanna's elbow and steered her toward the kitchen table along with her chagrined mother and uncle.

Once they were all seated, Ruth began. "Teddy, where is my piano?"

Teddy, who slumped in his chair like an 8th grader serving detention, pointed to Joanna with a tilt of his head. "Ask her."

"Joanna, where is my piano?" Ruth demanded. Joanna started to answer, but found her mouth had gone completely dry. She rose to get a glass of water. "Oh no, you don't!" Ruth pulled her back down to the wooden kitchen chair. "Answer my question!"

Joanna tried to work up enough saliva to unstick her tongue, cleared her throat and croaked out, "Gone."

"What do you mean, 'gone'?"

"I asked you about donations this morning, and you said I could donate the piano."

"I said you could give away the things in the bags, not the piano!" yelled Ruth.

Joanna felt her face flush. She couldn't look Ruth in the eye. "I'm sorry, Grandma. I guess I misunderstood."

"Well, there's no real harm done. I'm sure the pick up won't happen today. You can move it back into the house later." Joanna felt her stomach churn. Teddy slunk a little farther down in the chair as if he was attempting to slip under the table. Joanna was just about to tell Ruth the truth about the state of her piano, but Ruth's attention had turned to Teddy and Beverly.

"When will you two be able to act like adults around each other?"

Beverly, who had been sitting at the end of the table with arms crossed, her face in a deep scowl, said, "I'm sorry, Mom. I know I shouldn't let Teddy get to me. But, I had to fly out here because this jackass lost you in New York City," she motioned toward Teddy. "AND, then there's the dog!"

Joanna cringed. *Oh boy, here we go.*

"Hey, don't blame me! Ma loves that dog," Teddy defended himself.

"Well, I love cucumbers, but they give me heartburn," Beverly returned.

Teddy drew a breath to reply, but could only manage, "Huh?"

Beverly scoffed. "I'm trying to say that not everything we love is good for us."

Teddy said, "Well, Thanksgiving dinner would be good about now. Me and Ma got ready-made from the grocery. All we have to do is heat it up. We even got mashed potatoes. Oops! Sorry, Bevie. I forgot. They used to make you gag."

Joanna cringed, sensing a suppressed shudder from Beverly. *Teddy, you're in for it now.*

"Actually, I've already made a dinner reservation," said Beverly.

"Of course, you have," smirked Teddy. "No ready-made food for Bevie."

Ruth stomped her good foot again under the table. Teddy's mouth snapped shut.

Beverly continued as if there had only been the brief irritation of a fly buzzing by. "I only made the reservation for three. So…uh, Teddy what are your plans?"

"I'm happy to have dinner here," Joanna volunteered. She really just wanted to flee the situation any way possible.

"Beverly, cancel that reservation," Ruth said. "We have plenty of good food here."

"I guess we're staying here. Bev, you lose," Teddy mocked.

"Stop, Teddy. Set the table like a good boy." Ruth swayed forward in her chair and attempted to scoot herself to a better position to stand. "I'll get out the food and start heating it up."

Joanna jumped up. "Grandma, let me do it."

Ruth sighed. "All right, Dear. That is a good plan. I'm feeling rather tired today."

Beverly said, "Mother, I'm not surprised that you're tired. It must be difficult taking care of the house by yourself."

Subtle, Mom! Joanna thought dreading 'the talk' that she knew was coming.

"You're right. As soon as this foot's healed, things will be easier for me."

"Well, Mom, just how long do you plan to live in this house?"

Ruth glared at her daughter. "As long as I have breath in my body!"

Beverly looked slightly taken aback at the force of Ruth's response, but she seemed to brace herself and head back into the fray. "But don't you have friends who live at Shady Oaks? Wouldn't you like to live closer to them?"

"I can see them easily enough. Why, Teddy took me over this morning for our weekly game of Euchre."

"That's only once a week," Beverly returned. "You could have company more often if your friends lived right down the hall."

"Enough, Beverly!" All activity in the kitchen ceased.

After an awkward pause, Beverly opened her mouth to speak, but a glare from Ruth kept the silence.

Finally, Ruth stood and said, "I don't feel well. I'm going to my room." Joanna moved to her side to help her down the hall, but Ruth pushed her away and shuffled down the plastic runner leading to the back of the house. The creaking of hinges was followed by the slam of Ruth's bedroom door.

Teddy was the first to get up and bolt for the door. "I'm not waiting around for dinner. I'm going to Spike's. Thanks for nothing, Bevie."

Beverly sat at the table scowling. Joanna, stomach growling, nibbled at a piece of turkey, but slipped the rest of the food into the refrigerator and then retreated down the hall to her bedroom before Beverly could get a second wind and start in on her.

Joanna flopped on the bed. From where she lay she could just see some of the long, jagged remains of the piano poking out of the garbage can. She sighed and tried to think how she would tell Ruth the real fate of the piano. Yawning, she drew a hand to her mouth and winced. Ow! She blurted out as she rubbed her burning bicep. *Guess that axe was heavier than I thought.* Out of energy, she drifted off to sleep.

Chapter 21

The next morning, Joanna awoke just as the November sun peeked into her window. On the cluttered nightstand next to her bed, the alarm clock glared at her in bold red numbers. "8:15? Why am I awake so early? She moaned, rubbing her bleary eyes "*Just five more minutes*," she thought to herself as she rolled away from the clock. But, she couldn't fall back to sleep. Her stomach growled and she found herself annoyed with her mother for making her miss dinner the night before.

Joanna had never been an early riser, much to her mother's dismay. During her childhood, Beverly had been Joanna's human alarm clock. Every morning when the alarm blared out from the other side of her bedroom, Joanna managed to totter over and silence it, and then leap back into bed burying herself under her covers, knowing that her mother would soon be in to nag her awake.

When she was young, this morning ritual seemed to work out well for both of them. "Just five more minutes," Beverly would softly inform Joanna as she opened the bedroom curtains and leaned over to kiss Joanna's forehead, a kiss that Joanna looked forward to as a young girl.

But, the older Joanna got, the more she disliked her mother's interference in her morning slumber, and the less patient Beverly became with Joanna's morning lethargy. Away at college, Joanna relished her freedom from Beverly's morning control. But, there were times when Joanna was late to class or missed one entirely that she caught herself blaming her mother for not teaching her to get up on time.

Flustered by thoughts of her mother, Joanna could not re-settle herself. The typical morning sounds in Ruth's neighborhood pushed their way into her consciousness: a neighbor starting up a chainsaw somewhere down the street; a dog barking in the distance; the house creaking and pinging as the ancient furnace struggled to keep the house heated. But, there was an odd stillness that helped to clear Joanna's head and prompted her to get up.

Still half asleep, she staggered down the hall into the bathroom and sat down to pee. Perched on the pot, she tried to focus on the new day, and the breakfast she knew Ruth would have waiting for her. Joanna smiled. *Grandma never cares what time I get up.* She never felt judged by Ruth, especially over something as trivial as the time she decided to get out of bed. Every day Ruth greeted her with a hug and a kiss, ready to chat over Joanna's first food of the day.

She went to the kitchen expecting her hug, but Ruth was not there. All that greeted her this morning was a note on the kitchen table, penned in her mother's block lettering: OUT FOR A WALK. *That's weird. Grandma and Mom on a walk together?* Her mom was a power-walker in the true sense of the word: fast with a goofy-looking stride. Ruth, on the other hand, was a slow, meandering walker, partly due to old age, but mostly because of her interest in the smallest details around her like a new blossom or butterfly flitting past.

Joanna couldn't imagine what would prompt her mother to subject herself to one of Ruth's nature walks. Confused but intrigued, Joanna couldn't resist a peek out the window to witness it. However, there was nothing to be seen in the backyard or in the front. "Huh? Maybe they took the car?" A quick peek at the driveway killed that theory. Joanna tried to rationalize the scenario, but it made no sense. Standing in the middle of the kitchen, she pondered the situation: *The note says they're on a walk, but Grandma's shoes are at the backdoor, yesterday's dishes are still dirty in the sink, and today's dose of her meds are still in Grandma's pillbox.* Joanna called out, "Grandma? Mom?" Not really expecting an answer, she didn't get one.

Maybe they're at Teddy's? But, Joanna quickly dismissed that idea based on last night's dispute and the fact that Peanut moped in the backyard, acting like he hadn't been fed. "Nice, Teddy," Joanna said condescendingly toward Teddy's house. And, then added,

"I'll be out in a minute, Peanut," not that either of them could hear her.

The hunger pangs growling in her stomach prompted Joanna to grab a granola bar and some milk. Sitting at the table and wearing a furl across her brow, Joanna turned her head as she heard voices outside. "Finally!" Joanna said, feeling relieved. The voices sounded happy, one laughing at something the other had just said. As she waited for Ruth and Beverly to enter through the back door, she started nervously tapping her foot.

It was hard to discern the particulars of the conversation, as the voices seemed to be moving farther away from, rather than toward, the house. Perplexed, Joanna walked into the living room to peer out the front window. Two middle-aged ladies, each holding a coffee mug and wearing too-tight workout attire, were walking past the house.

She spun around, intent on going back to the kitchen, when she noticed Ruth's bedroom door closed at the end of the hallway. *Grandma never closes her door, unless she's asleep. And, why is she still asleep at 8:30?*

Joanna tiptoed down the hall and stood outside of Ruth's door. Not really wanting to disturb her grandmother, but thinking Ruth would most certainly want to be up by now, "Grandma?" she whispered. Joanna worried that last night's squabble had been too hard on Ruth. Wondering if she should just let her grandmother sleep, Joanna instead decided to rap lightly on the bedroom door and ask if Ruth knew what time it was. When her knock received no answer, Joanna knocked again, and then turned the knob, trying to open the door as quietly as she could. The door let out a pathetic creak. Like other things in Ruth's house, it had not received good care over the years. *Ever hear of WD-40, Grandma?* Joanna grunted as she used the weight of her body to push her way into the room. Perhaps some junk Grandma kept behind the door had fallen. "Grandma?" Joanna inquired again into the darkened room, sure that her noisy entrance had woken Ruth. But, there was no answer.

Once inside the room, it took a moment for Joanna's eyes to adjust. She squinted at the bed, expecting her grandmother to be there, but it was obviously empty. Puzzled by her grandmother's absence, she stood her ground, wondering where in the world Ruth could be. Absent-mindedly, Joanna checked behind the door to see what had impeded her entry. Startled, she jumped at what appeared to be a figure lying on the floor. "Oh, crap!" Heart racing, she poked at it with a toe to prove to herself that her imagination had not gotten the better of her, then reached down to further assess the situation.

As soon as Joanna grasped the solid form, she recoiled and bolted upright. There on the floor in front of her lay her grandmother face up, eyes gazing at the ceiling with her dress draped around her legs. Ruth looked content, but even in the dim light of the bedroom, Joanna could see an eerie cast to Ruth's skin.

Her eyes, usually so full of love and life, were fixed in a lifeless stare, although the expression on Ruth's face was one of peace.

Stunned as she was by her discovery, Joanna became swept up in her feelings for her grandmother. Kneeling down, she took Ruth's left hand in her own. It was oddly limp and didn't return Joanna's grip. She slid her fingers to Ruth's wrist. Finding no pulse confirmed what she already knew. "Oh, Grandma."

In her grief, Joanna lost track of everything around her, so much so that she failed to hear the sound of keys hitting the kitchen table, the opening and closing of the refrigerator door, and her mother calling her name. It wasn't until Beverly was standing in the hallway right outside of Ruth's bedroom demanding to know why Joanna was on the floor that Joanna felt the lack of circulation in her legs and the tears on her cheeks.

"What in the world are you doing on the floor, Joanna? And, why did you let Grandma sleep so...." Beverly's voice trailed off as Joanna looked up at her pathetically. "Jojo? What's the matter?" Beverly's voice softened as she took in Joanna's appearance and then she gasped as she took in the entirety of the scene. "Mom?" Beverly pleaded hopelessly.

The EMTs were professional, yet compassionate, as they checked Ruth for vital signs and then confirmed what Joanna and

Beverly already knew to be true. Eric, the head paramedic, said, "I'm sorry, Ma'am. She's gone."

Grabbing his arm, Beverly pled, "So, what do we do now?"

"I need her doctor's phone number, Ma'am," he replied calmly.

"I'll get it, Mom," Joanna offered as she headed toward the kitchen.

Eric made a quick call to Ruth's doctor to verify that she would agree to sign the death certificate. "Okay, thank you, Dr. Janice." He hung up the phone and turned to face Beverly. "Ma'am, we got her permission. You can call the funeral home of your choice and have Mrs. Lathrop transferred there. Sorry for your loss."

As Joanna watched the paramedics maneuver the empty gurney through Ruth's cramped living room, a strange thought popped into her head. *Good thing I got rid of that piano.*

Chapter 22

Lost in thought, Joanna jumped at the sound of her mother's voice. "Joanna, did you hear me?" Beverly was snapping her fingers at Joanna in an effort to catch her attention.

"What, Mom?" Joanna responded flatly with neither interest nor sarcasm.

"If you'd get your head out of the sand, you would have heard me the first three times. I said that I'm going over to the funeral home to make the arrangements. You stay here and get your things straightened up." Beverly furled her brow and muttered, "I swear you're getting to be more and more like your grandmother all the time."

Taking her mother's comment as a compliment, a faint smile lit Joanna's face for a moment.

"Joanna, did you hear me?"

"Yes, I'm coming with you."

"No, that's not what I said. You stay here and get packed. We're leaving tonight."

Frowning, Joanna repeated, "We're leaving tonight?"

"Joanna, you know I can't be away from home for very long. Houses don't sell themselves you know." Beverly paused, grinning slightly to herself as she slipped into her coat. Joanna sighed at her mother's self-perceived cleverness.

Reaching for her own coat, Joanna tried to recall details about the handful of funerals she had attended in her lifetime, remembering that all of those ceremonies were quite involved and had happened over the course of several days. *How can Grandma's funeral happen in one day?* she wondered.

"Mom, do you really think we can pull Grandma's funeral together this afternoon?"

"Well, of course not, Joanna. There's no time for any of that. I'm going to make arrangements to have Grandma cremated. When I talked to the funeral director, he said all I need to do is go over today, sign some papers and pay for the whole thing, and that he would take care of everything else so that we can go home."

Joanna pondered her mother's plan. *But wait, how are we going to let everyone know about a funeral service?* Joanna was baffled; she simply could not figure out how they were going to cram three days' worth of bereavement into one afternoon and still make it to the airport for an evening flight.

As Beverly continued to ready herself for the trip to the funeral home, it suddenly struck Joanna that Teddy, Ruth's only son, might not even know about the tragedy.

"But what about Teddy, Mom? Don't you think we should ask him what he wants for Grandma?"

"Really, Joanna? Teddy doesn't even know what he wants to do with his own life. This is not a decision he needs to be part of."

"But, Mom, Grandma was his mother too," Joanna reasoned. And then, watching as her mother prepared to leave the house, Joanna pleaded, "And, what about me? I need time to say goodbye to Grandma. You're not the only one this has had an impact on, you know. And, what about all of Grandma's friends? And, what about Dad? And, Nana Jackman? They all loved her too. They'll all want a chance to say goodbye."

Getting no response, Joanna followed her mother out the back door and into the driveway. With her voice rising, Joanna persisted, "And, what about what Grandma wanted?

Rummaging through her purse, Beverly extracted the keys and opened the car door.

Feeling disregarded, Joanna yelled, "Mom! Are you listening to me?"

Keys in hand, Beverly turned toward Joanna. Hoping she had her mother's full attention, Joanna said, "You can't just ignore everyone else for your own convenience. This isn't just about whether or not you can sell another house. This is about Grandma. She was amazing and a lot of people really cared about her, and they deserve to have the time to say goodbye the way

Grandma wanted it to be." Joanna stood, defiantly facing her mother, arms crossed over her chest.

"Joanna, that's all fine and good, but there is simply no time. And, there aren't really that many people who would attend anyway."

"Really, Mom? How would you even know?" Joanna continued her tirade. "You never spent any time here. It was like you were ashamed of Grandma. You don't know anything about her or what she was like or want she wanted. You were her daughter, but you didn't really know her. I don't think you even really liked her."

"Alright, Joanna. That's enough. I know this is hard on you. And, whether you believe it or not, it's hard on me, too. Let's not make it any more difficult than it has to be, okay? A quick cremation without the fuss of a service will be easier on everyone. You'll see."

"Maybe easier for you, Mom, but not for me! Not for Teddy! Not for anybody else!" The words spewed from Joanna hysterically.

"Joanna, calm down. It's not that big of a deal. People are cremated all the time. It's a perfectly honorable way to pay last respects to someone."

But, Joanna refused to calm down. "Mom, this isn't just someone. This is Grandma! And, we need to have a traditional funeral for her!" Tears welled up in her eyes. Her voice cracked.

"We need to give her friends a chance to come and talk to us about how wonderful Grandma is…or was."

"Look, Joanna, I am not going to stand around and pretend like I owe these people anything."

"These people! Who are you talking about? Your brother? Grandma's loyal friends? And, what do you mean by 'pretend,' Mom? There is nothing to pretend about. We do owe these people. We owe them for being so good to Grandma, and to Teddy, all these years. We owe them for loving Grandma. We owe them the decency to say goodbye to Ruth Lathrop, their friend."

"Well, I am having her cremated. End of discussion." Beverly paused, smoothed her skirt, and took a deep breath. "Now, I am leaving for the funeral home. You can come with me if you want to, or you can stay here. It doesn't really matter whether…."

Without waiting for her mother to finish, Joanna said, "Oh right, it always has to be your way." In an effort to make her disgust at her mother known, Joanna stormed across the driveway, flung open the back door of the house and slammed it so hard that it sent one of the panes in the porch light crashing to the ground. Beverly drove away.

Chapter 23

Upset and with no plan, Joanna flew out of Ruth's house. She found herself on Teddy's front stoop, knocking and ringing the bell simultaneously. *I cannot believe she is so self-centered,* Joanna seethed. *It's not like Grandma is some bum off the street. It's her own mother!* While she fumed, Joanna took her frustration out on Teddy's entryway, pressing and holding the bell, producing a constant concert of ding dongs until it was interrupted by the sound of the lock and the door creaking open.

"Hey, take it easy on the doorbell, would you?" Teddy mumbled as he opened the door. Obviously fresh out of bed, he scratched himself and rubbed his eyes, while trying to focus on the rude person on his front step.

"Oh, sorry," Joanna muttered. "Did you hear the bad news?" she added sadly.

One hand on the door and the other massaging his forehead, Teddy squinted through the bright sun at Joanna. "Bevie, *texted* me this morning."

"Oh, that's just like Mom. She couldn't even bother to pick up the phone. She drives me crazy. It's always all about her. Everything has to be *her* way. Everybody is supposed to do what *she* wants. Like this cremation. What's up with that? She always treats Grandma like she's an embarrassment. Mom's always trying to wrap up loose ends. Now she's even trying to make death into a neat little package!" Joanna stopped her tirade and stared at Teddy expectantly. "Well, are you going to invite me in?"

"Yeah, come in, but take off your shoes." Teddy shuffled over to his dated, but immaculate Lazy-Boy in the corner of his living room. Absentmindedly, he reached for the remote and hit 'power.' The large flat screen TV began to blare out something about 'November's playmate…' prompting Teddy to glance over at Joanna and then nonchalantly change to the cartoon channel.

Engrossed in the antics of Popeye and Olive Oyl, Teddy placed the remote on the end table, grabbed the Lazy-Boy lever, and extended the footrest on his chair, reclining himself comfortably.

Glancing around the room for something on which she could sit, Joanna realized that she could not recall having ever been in Teddy's living room. The austere orderliness of his home, which was in direct opposition to Ruth's disorganized abode, surprised her. Other than the recliner in which he sat, Teddy's living room had only two other pieces of furniture. An end table sitting next to the Lazy-Boy was topped with a crocheted doily and a

Thirstystone Coaster. In the center of the room, in front of where a couch might have been, had Teddy owned one, sat a pristinely empty coffee table. Teddy's sparse living room contained no other seating; therefore, Joanna sat down on the coffee table and faced Teddy.

"So, Teddy…" Joanna started.

"Hey, what are you doing?" Teddy hollered. Joanna jumped at the loud volume of Teddy's pointed query. "Geez, Joanna! What, were you raised in a barn? There's a chair in the kitchen. Go get it."

Joanna leaped up off the coffee table and dutifully entered the kitchen to retrieve a chair.

"Hey, and watch the floor in there, I just waxed," Teddy yelled across the tiny living room at her.

Teddy's kitchen looked like something straight out of a 1950's diner: sleek and covered in plastic. The room was tidy; it had a place for everything and everything was in its place. Joanna noted the sheen on the floor as she carefully lifted a chair, making sure not to drag it or bump it into anything. Re-entering the living room, she smiled at Teddy as she positioned the chair in front of him. In her awe at Teddy's immaculate home, Joanna felt compelled to pay him a compliment, but before she could get the words out of her mouth, Teddy bellowed, "Hey, move it over. You're blocking my view!"

Joanna raised her eyebrows, drew in a deep breath, and scooted her chair out of his line of vision. "So nice to see you. Won't you have a seat, Joanna?" she muttered disparagingly.

"Yeah, well no one invited you over here, you know."

"Yep, you're right," Joanna agreed. "But, I'm here and the least you could do is pretend like you're glad to see me." She sighed. "So, anyway, have you heard about my mother's stupid plan to have a quick cremation without a fuss?"

"Sounds like Bevie. She's always been uptight and impatient," Teddy interjected. Still gazing at Popeye, he continued, "Are you calling the plan stupid, or…" Then he nodded his head and stroked his chin philosophically, as he gazed momentarily at Joanna and said, "What do you *really* think about your mom?" before he returned his attention to the TV.

Confused yet intrigued by Teddy's question, Joanna blurted out, "What do you mean, what do I think about my mom?" Then, she paused and frowned as she contemplated just what she did think about her mother. "Well, you know Mom," she began hesitantly. "She's always right. She's always well dressed. Her business is successful. She does everything perfectly. No one can measure up to her standards, but everyone wants to be just like her."

Joanna gave a quick nod of her head to punctuate the sense of satisfaction she felt about the answer she had just given. She waited for Teddy's response, anticipating complete agreement or at least a grunt of approval.

"*I* don't want to be just like her," Teddy announced point blank.

Joanna drew in a breath, preparing to throw Teddy a zinger, *Yeah, you would look pretty funny in her high heels*, but then she realized Teddy was serious and that his comment was more than skin deep.

"Yeah, but…" was her first attempt at a rebuttal. But, as Joanna tried to wrap her head around Teddy's proclamation, her thoughts became more muddled. *Teddy and Mom don't see eye to eye. That's no secret. But, everyone really does admire Mom. Why wouldn't Teddy want what Mom has?* Joanna's face crinkled as she looked up and to the right, then up and to the left, contemplating Teddy's comment. *Is Teddy actually saying that he liked himself the way he was? Is he really content with his life, and with himself?*

"So, what are you trying to say, Teddy? That you like that people don't take you seriously and that you're out of work and that you depend on Grandma for everything?"

And, even though Joanna recognized the tone of rudeness laced into her questions, Teddy didn't seem to take any offense. He simply answered her by countering with his own set of questions, "So, Joanna, what you're trying to say is that you like that people don't see you as responsible, that you don't follow through on things, and that you can't admit that you are struggling so much that you were thinking of ending it all in the lake?"

Joanna grimaced and stared directly at Teddy who still appeared wrapped up in the wonderful world of cartoons. "No, it's not like that at all. I'm an adult. I take responsibility for my failures," Joanna paused and then quickly added, "and my successes."

"That's good. Glad to hear it." Teddy said noncommittally. "I may not have everything in life figured out, but I am what I am…" He turned to face Joanna straight on. And then, pushing his sleeve up and baring his right bicep, he continued in his best Popeye imitation, "And that's all that I yam. A-gah-gah-gah-gah-gah-gah!"

Joanna was stunned. As she gazed at her uncle, drop-jawed, trying to figure out how to respond to what he had just said, Teddy appeared oblivious to the impact his words were having on her. As a matter of fact, he seemed oblivious to everything except for the oversized TV screen directly in front of him. Without so much as a goodbye, Joanna rose from her chair, carried it into the kitchen, and slipped unnoticed out the front door, not knowing what to do or where to go.

Chapter 24

Head throbbing, Joanna contemplated this newfound wisdom about her uncle as she absentmindedly descended Teddy's front steps. She wore a frown furled across her brow as she walked to nowhere in particular. Her mind raced. *Teddy actually likes himself? He takes pride in his home? He's figured out how to be happy with himself?* She stopped walking. "I don't get it," she blurted out. She was baffled. She couldn't seem to help herself understand what her uncle had disclosed about himself. Inhaling deeply, Joanna let out an enormous sigh as she continued to think through this revelation.

With each step she took, thoughts churned and confusion ensued. Her entire life, Joanna had heard how irresponsible Teddy was, and she had just spent the last few days witnessing how disgusting he could be. *He's a big slob who acts like a kid most of the time. His friends are sleazy. And, he relies on other people, like Grandma, to bail him out. He might just be the laziest person I know, but that scuzzball is enjoying life more than I am.*

Joanna stopped again and exclaimed, "I don't get it."

And then, a kernel of a notion popped into her head, much like the Grinch when he realizes that destroying the Whos' presents will not actually destroy their Christmas.

Teddy seems to be happy. Grandma was certainly happy. Even Mom's happy in her own way. So…what's my problem? I should be happy. I'm young. I'm fairly smart. My family has money.

"Aaaa!" Joanna erupted in frustration. "I'm so confused! Why am I not happy?" Her lower lip quivered as tears welled up. *How come everyone else has it so figured out?* As she pondered her predicament, Joanna's shoulders shook as she moaned, "What is wrong with me?"

Closing her eyes, she sobbed, wondering why she was the only idiot who didn't have her life in order. With tears flowing down her face, she reached into her pocket, pulled out a Kleenex, and blew her nose.

Just then a car backed out of the driveway across the street. Suddenly embarrassed, as she realized she wasn't alone, Joanna sniffed and quickly wiped her eyes. The driver tapped her horn and gave Joanna a friendly wave, then sped away. Faking a smile, Joanna waved back.

As she witnessed the driver's departure from the neighborhood, a solution to her own predicament occurred to her. *I'll just go back to school.* But then, acknowledging how avoidance was her typical modus operandi, she started to cry again as she admitted to herself, *But, then I'll just be running away again.* She sniffled as sadness cast its shadow across her face once again and an exceptionally large tear made its way slowly down her cheek.

Deflated by the admission that she wasn't able to stick around and deal with the things life had to throw at her, Joanna inhaled several times, trying to control her runny nose. Her eyes felt puffy, her nose felt raw, and her head throbbed. *What am I going to do?* Joanna asked herself again. She just felt stuck. Just as she thought her head would explode from thinking and crying, her cell phone rang. Through blurry eyes, she saw that it was Deborah. Her first reaction was to ignore the call, but then she decided to pick up.

Joanna heard the upbeat voice of her roommate on the other end of the line.

"Hey, Jo! How's things with you, Seesta'?"

Joanna tried to return Deborah's greeting, but the words stuck in her throat. Instead of speaking, all Joanna could manage was a pathetic kind of slurping sound.

To Joanna's lack of response, Deborah called out worriedly, "Joanna? Are you there?"

"Yep," was all Joanna could manage.

"Hey, Jo. What's wrong?"

Joanna tried to collect her thoughts. So much had happened to her that she didn't know where to start or how to tell Deborah what she was feeling. The grief and emotions she had held in check since she found Ruth dead on the floor were flying around in her head: the anger she felt at her mother weighing her down, her confusion with Teddy's newly revealed reflection, not to mention her frustration with her own lack of ability to cope. So many thoughts were racing through her mind that she couldn't speak, while at the same time, everything was waiting to spill out of her, needing to be told to someone else.

"Grandma is dead." It was the first time Joanna had actually said it out loud, and for some reason, it had a temporary calming effect on her.

"Oh, Joanna. I'm so sorry."

"Yeah, she just got old, I guess. But, you know what, Deb. Grandma had a happy life. Even though she got messier as she got older, I think she is one of the happiest people I've ever known." Joanna paused as she smiled to herself at the thought of her grandmother.

"But, then," she continued with more gusto, "there's my mother." She paused as the anger inside of her percolated. "My mom can always just….make me so…mad!...You know?" Joanna growled into the phone. She tried to regain her composure as she spoke but was failing at it miserably. As tears once again collected in her eyes, she covered her face with her free hand, and then wiped her nose on her sleeve.

"All my life, I always thought that there was something wrong with me. That my mom didn't give a damn about me. That she wasn't really proud of me or something." Joanna's thoughts gained momentum, and she became more agitated.

"I don't know. She's just such a strong person, someone who I could never measure up to. Everything about her is perfect from her hair to her clothes to her job. Hell, you've seen our living room." Joanna chuckled and sputtered through her words. "How could any kid feel normal growing up there?" she joked.

Deborah laughed.

"And, then there's Grandma." She paused and gazed across the horizon as if Ruth was standing there. "Oh, Deb," she continued wistfully, "you can really not even imagine how much stuff Grandma has. Or, well, had. She had so much stuff she didn't even know what stuff she had anymore. It wasn't always this bad, but it just kept getting worse. And, everything is SO disorganized. Hell, how could any kid feel normal growing up there? Joanna gestured with her hands as she made the comparison between herself and her mother, laughing in spite of how she was feeling.

"Wow, talk about two total opposites," Deborah offered.

"Yeah, I know. But, the funny thing is, Deb, Grandma just didn't seem to care what you thought about her. She was just glad to see you. She always made me feel so special, even though I didn't think that I was. And, Mom, the one person who should have made me feel special was always so concerned with appearances—how I looked, how I dressed, who I hung out with.

It's always how it should be with her, not how it is. It's just so frustrating."

As Joanna contemplated her next statement, she heard Deborah yell, "Hold on a minute, Mom. Sorry, Joanna. Be right back."

Feeling somewhat ignored, Joanna said, "Sure. No problem." But to herself she thought, *No problem, I'm just baring my soul here!*

As she waited, Joanna heard Deborah in the background having a discussion with her mother. "Sorry, Mom, I can't do that right now. I'm talking to Joanna. I'll help you as soon as I get off the phone."

Deborah returned to the phone, "I'm back."

"Your Mom is so nice. My mom never takes no for an answer."

"It's no big deal. She knows I'll follow through when I get off the phone."

"You're so lucky. There's no making my mom wait. Everything has to be done right now. I guess that's what's really bugging me, Deb. She's just all about quickly tying up Grandma's life and moving on. I mean I do think that she's really sad that Grandma's gone, but..."

"Yeah, well, your mom is a lot more practical than she is sentimental, Jo."

"Yeah, I know, but a few days ago, Grandma actually talked to me about how she wanted things arranged at her funeral after she died. She told me the list of songs she wanted sung, and the Bible verses she wanted read. She even wrote down a list of food she wanted people to have after the ceremony. She said she just wanted to make sure that everyone would have a good time. It was kind of creepy, almost like she knew it was going to happen."

"Well, she was kind of old, so it's not that surprising," Deborah offered.

"No, you're right, but what was so surprising is that however chaotically Grandma lived her life, she seemed so organized about all of the stuff she wanted for the people who came to her funeral. She even showed me the dress that she wanted to be buried in and the necklace too." Joanna paused and then trying to imitate Ruth, she said, "But don't leave my jewelry on me when I'm six feet under. I want you to have it, dear." Joanna smiled and sighed. "She called me 'dear' a lot."

"That's nice," Deborah said. And then when Joanna didn't reply, she asked, "So, how are you coming with the funeral plans?"

"What do you mean?" Joanna asked.

"What do you mean, what do I mean? Your Grandma practically planned her own funeral. All she needs now is for you to carry out her last request."

"Well, yeah, that would be nice if I could, but Mom's already signed off on Grandma's cremation and bought our plane tickets back to Chicago. There isn't going to be any funeral service."

"Oh?" was Deborah's surprised reply.

"Well, it's not like I can override my mother. I'm just the granddaughter. For all I know, Grandma's ashes have already been sealed up in some fancy urn Mom picked out. Nothing but the best for Beverly, don't you know."

"So?"

"So, what?"

"So, your grandma left you one thing to do after she died and now you're not going to do it?"

"Hey, no fair. It's not my fault. Mom took over the second she got here. Thanks a lot, Deborah. I thought you would understand."

"I do understand and as your friend, I know how horrible you're going to feel later if you don't carry out your grandmother's wishes. She was depending on you."

"Yeah, she picked a real winner, didn't she?"

"Yes, she did." Deborah paused, and when Joanna didn't respond she asked again, "so…?

"So nothing. I'm tired, I'm done, and I am outta here. Talk to ya later." And, with cynicism dripping off her last words to Deborah, she hung up.

As soon as she had done it, she felt horrible. Deborah was her best friend and possibly her only ally at the moment. She contemplated calling back, but the shame she felt at her lack of self-control prevented her from doing so.

Standing there in the middle of the sidewalk, grief, anger, and self-pity pervaded Joanna's mood. She started to cry again. *Why did you have to leave me, Grandma?* She sobbed and plodded along the path back to Ruth's house. *You were the only one who really loved me. Without you around to tell me that I'm good enough, I don't think I can face school or my parents or even my life.* Joanna, eyes blurry with tears, wailed, "I just don't want to be here."

Out of nowhere she felt a hard smack in the face. "Ow!" She rubbed her cheek as she realized that she had walked straight into a low hanging tree branch. "Figures," she muttered. "I can't even walk right."

Lost in her sorrowful thoughts, and still focused on her stinging cheek, Joanna sniffled. "I've got to get out of here."

An abrupt but gentle autumn breeze blew across Joanna's face, followed by a cascade of dry leaves enveloping her in an unexpected sense of calm. At just that moment, to Joanna, a simple act of nature felt like an embrace from her grandmother, as though Ruth was speaking through the wind saying, "I'm here, sweetie. I'll always be with you. And, you can do anything you want, don't you know."

Joanna knew that she was putting her own emotions into a mere meteorological phenomenon, but she felt comforted none-the-less as she let a sense of well-being wash over her. With happy assurances from her grandmother tucked into her head, Joanna strolled back to the house.

The house felt eerily empty and intensely quiet. Had Ruth been at home, she would have offered Joanna some words of encouragement along with some piping hot tea in a chipped cup. Joanna put on the teakettle for herself, and in spite of her gloomy feelings, she smiled to herself at the thought of her grandmother.

Sipping peach tea, one of her favorites, Joanna contemplated her dilemma—go along with her mother's directives or honor her grandmother's last wishes. Deborah's questions resonated in her head: *What was she going to do about her grandmother's wishes? What could she do?* At the very least, she could send a text to Deborah to say she was sorry. She typed the message, "sorry D thx for being my gd friend."

Chapter 25

The sun shone merrily through the enormous stained glass windows of the modest church Ruth had attended her entire life. Despite looking dreary, weathered and every bit its century-plus age, the church was an adequate structure for its dwindling population of worshippers, now reduced by one at Ruth's passing.

Seated in the front pew, Joanna noted the tired altar decor and the barren walls in need of paint, which seemed to sag into further dismay as the octogenarian choir members clucked and cackled through their version of "What a Friend We Have In Jesus." *Surely, Jesus isn't feeling friendly about that noise*, Joanna thought as she slouched in her hard, wooden seat. *I hope this goes well.*

In spite of her discomfort, a sense of contentment stirred in Joanna simply because she was in a place that Ruth had frequented. Instead of dwelling on herself, Joanna focused on the multitude of people crammed into the little church on such short notice. Teddy and his less-than-savory friends had been instrumental in getting the word out to everyone. The crowd's willingness to show up at the spur-of-the-moment confirmed for

Joanna what a wonderful person Ruth had been, not just to her granddaughter, but also to what seemed like everyone in central New Jersey.

And, so, here we are, Joanna thought. Deborah's challenge – insisting that she carry out Ruth's last wishes – had inspired Joanna to plan the memorial tribute that her beloved grandmother had requested and deserved in spite of Beverly's focus on quickly sending Ruth off to heaven in an urn.

A multitude of flowers, wind chimes, and stuffed animals adorned and overwhelmed the church altar. A large picture of Ruth as a much younger woman, which Joanna had found among Ruth's many possessions, smiled down at the crowd from an easel standing near the pulpit. Since Ruth had been cremated, Joanna placed next to her portrait, the dress, necklace and earrings Ruth had designated as her burial outfit.

As boxes of tissue were passed around among the gathered mourners, the service commenced. The church choir, standing in their pews at the side of the altar, began with their shrill, yet heartfelt, rendition of "The Old Rugged Cross." Joanna smiled and sighed, *I hope you like it, Grandma.*

When the hymn ended, the minister said a brief greeting and then called for anyone who wanted to speak. Hands shot up all over the sanctuary.

"Ruth Lathrop was my neighbor for 55 years, but I have to tell you, she felt just like family to me."

"Ruth always had a smile on her face, and she always had a kind word to say."

The verbal accolades about Ruth went on and on. It seemed like everyone wanted their turn to say something about the remarkable woman they all knew and loved. There were so many comments that finally the minister felt compelled to jump in.

"Well, it is certainly easy to tell that Mrs. Lathrop was well loved by all of us. How about we wrap up these wonderful comments…"

Suddenly, Percy who had been sitting right next to Teddy sprang from his seat and cleared his throat. "She was just like a mother to me. I never had anybody care about me so much," he mumbled, then sat down and loudly honked his runny nose into a Kleenex. It was the only serious and heartfelt comment Joanna had ever heard from him.

"Thank you, everybody. Now Teddy, Ruth's son, would like to say a few words"

As Teddy ambled up to the lectern, Joanna's stomach tightened. *Teddy speaking publically was not part of the plan.*

"Well, yeah, I would like say somethin'," Teddy roughly cleared his throat. "So…uh…Ma was the best ma anybody could ask for. She took real good care of me and Bevie and raised us good. Isn't that right, Bevie?"

Joanna felt Beverly's body stiffen as she inhaled faintly and gave Teddy a slight nod.

With phlegm rattling in his throat, Teddy continued, "Ma lived her own way...Uh...she was always concerned with everybody else...and... she made them feel special." Teddy rubbed his nose, and then glanced up toward the ceiling as if in deep thought.

While the silence continued, Joanna wondered, *Is he done or just stuck?* But, before anyone could rescue him, he cleared his throat and started again. "Uh...She had no enemies, she regretted nothing, and she managed to make the most of whatever she was given." Pausing yet again, Teddy dragged his hand up his nose and over his forehead, finishing in his hair. "Uh, Ma only took what little she needed and gave back more in return." Teddy hesitated, took a breath, and then choked out, "Ma was great that way."

As the sniffling and nose blowing in the crowd started up again in earnest, Teddy wiped his nose on his sleeve. He ended with a quiver in his voice, "Well, I guess that's it."

Joanna felt her mother's shoulders begin to shake ever so slightly, as Teddy ambled back to his seat. Sneaking a peek at Beverly, she saw tears glistening on her face. Up until that point, Joanna had held it together, but her mother's reaction to her brother's heartfelt words was more than she could take. Tears welled up in her own eyes.

Noticing that Beverly's hand was lying loosely across her immaculately pressed tweed skirt, Joanna felt a sudden urge to reach out and hold her mother's hand. But, she couldn't move. *What I am so afraid of? The worst she can do is – what – pull her hand away? And, she won't do that. What would people think?* Joanna pondered the simple act that was proving to be a major gut-wrenching decision for her. *You know, I don't really care. I need Mom to hold my hand.*

Joanna put thinking aside and simply slipped her hand into her mom's, just as a young child might do. And, even though Beverly didn't really return the clasp, Joanna felt solace in her mother's touch. But, she was taken aback as she felt her mother move her hand, push Joanna's hand off of her lap, and then shift and move her body away. Joanna's feeling of euphoria dwindled.

But then, Joanna felt her mother's arm cradle around her shoulder and hold on tight in a comforting embrace. "This is just what Grandma would have wanted, Joanna. And, it's just what I needed. I just didn't know it. Thank you, sweetie, this is perfect."

And, Joanna smiled.

Acknowledgements

To Elizabeth Nierman, our editor: thank you for your thoughtful feedback and for utilizing your literary background in a way that brought meaningful insight and a fresh perspective to our work.

To Jim Streed and Jeff Wojtowicz, our husbands: our special thanks to you both for believing in us and encouraging us throughout this writing process. Your unconditional support inspires us.

About the Authors

Patricia Shinn Wojtowicz

is a retired college professor currently working as a stained glass artist in the Chicago area. *Relative Disenchantment*, her first novel, focuses on the multi-generational relationship of a college student, mother and, grandmother. Patricia's past experiences with her remarkable grandmothers and her current relationships with her amazing grandsons influence her as a writer.

Christine Petersen Streed

is twice retired—first as a physical therapist and then as a communications director. She started writing while working in her professions and has been published in national trade journals and in local magazines. *Relative Disenchantment* is her debut novel. She lives in the Chicago area with her husband.

Made in the USA
Lexington, KY
28 February 2017